SF

D0856394

THE KILLER
OF CIBECUE

Center Point
Large Print

Also by Nelson C. Nye and available from
Center Point Large Print:

Born to Trouble

THE KILLER OF CIBECUE

Nelson C. Nye

CENTER POINT LARGE PRINT
THORNDIKE, MAINE

This Center Point Large Print edition
is published in the year 2016 by arrangement with
Golden West Literary Agency.

First US edition: Greenberg Publishing Co.
First UK edition: Nicholson and Watson.

The text of this Large Print edition is unabridged.
In other aspects, this book may vary
from the original edition.
Printed in the United States of America
on permanent paper.
Set in 16-point Times New Roman type.

ISBN: 978-1-68324-045-7 (hardcover)
ISBN: 978-1-68324-049-5 (paperback)

Library of Congress Cataloging-in-Publication Data

Names: Nye, Nelson C. (Nelson Coral), 1907–1997, author.
Title: The killer of Cibecue / Nelson C. Nye.
Description: Center Point Large Print edition. | Thorndike, Maine :
Center Point Large Print, 2016. | ©1936
Identifiers: LCCN 2016014682| ISBN 9781683240457 (hardcover : alk.
paper) | ISBN 9781683240495 (pbk. : alk. paper)
Subjects: LCSH: Large type books. | GSAFD: Western stories.
Classification: LCC PS3527.Y33 K55 2016 | DDC 813/.54—dc23
LC record available at http://lccn.loc.gov/2016014682

For
Eugene Cunningham

THE KILLER OF CIBECUE

1

"Good evening, Dan."

As Dorinda Broughton stepped into the Sheriff's Office at Cibecue, she smiled. She was tall and willowy, an olive-skinned creature with sun-tanned cheeks and a dash of midnight in her hair. On most occasions her eyes were clear and blue and level. They were blue and level now, but in their depths was a vague troubled light which the young officer of the law, rising from his chair, was quick to note.

"Howdy, Dorinda. Long time no see."

So far as she was able to determine, Dan Stuart's face underwent no change in expression. Her appearance at his temporary office seemed to bring him neither pleasure nor regret. Surely, as a lover, his attitude left something to be desired.

He was a tall young man, this newly-elected sheriff; a bronzed product of the cow country, long of leg, narrow-hipped, and broad of shoulder. A man in the depths of whose agate glance might be detected a lurking glint of sardonic humor. He was not, the girl believed, the sort of person with whom ordinary folk would care to trifle. But then, Caspar Druce could in no sense be considered ordinary. No man who could do what he'd been doing could ever be so described.

As usual, young Stuart was clad in faded Levi's tucked into hand-stitched range boots. His curly yellow hair, so often hidden beneath the black Stetson laying beside his desk, was rumpled. As usual, too, the blue flannel shirt beneath his open pinto vest was scrupulously clean. The dark crossed gunbelts sagged in their habitual place about his narrow hips, their Colt-filled holsters thonged to his sturdy legs.

Gazing on him now, as he stood beside his desk unsmiling, Dorinda realized what most citizens of Navajo County had long contended: Dan Stuart was something of a mystery. He had a tantalizing habit of keeping himself and his thoughts strictly to himself—even she knew little of what went on in the alert mind behind those level agate eyes.

"No, I've been pretty busy at home these last few weeks," she said. "What with calf round-up coming on and all, I've had my hands full helping Dad. This talk of war between the sheep and cattle interests is getting more noisy all the time. Do you think they'll really fight?"

The sheriff shook his head. His square jaw looked suddenly grim, she thought, and the smooth-shaven lips above it seemed determined.

"But if it should come to war, which side would you back?" she asked hesitantly.

Dan Stuart smiled suddenly, and his eyes twinkled as he countered:

"There'll be no war in Cibecue Valley, Dorinda."

"But—but my father thinks there will. And—and—" the vague troubled light in her fine blue eyes seemed to grow more definite, "and Jabe says if the sheepmen break camp at Picture Rock and try to cross the valley, things will tear loose that can't be stopped without gun-play."

"Yeah, Jabe goes pretty strong on war talk," Stuart agreed, "but I wouldn't put too much stock in it, was I you. The older hands in this valley ain't anxious for another repetition of the Tonto Basin fracas. Pleasant Valley was bloody enough. There'll be no war in the Cibecue."

"I wish I could feel as certain of it as you are," she said, somberly. "When do you think Hoskins' people will be moving in?"

Hoskins was secretary for the Tucumcari Pool, an out-of-state organization concerning whom there was a deal of speculation going on in Cibecue Valley.

Stuart's smile faded out. An odd expression flickered momentarily in his eyes and was gone. "I wouldn't know."

"Well, I just stopped in to say 'Howdy' while I was in town," Dorinda murmured casually. "I guess I'd better be getting on home. Why," with a glance at her wrist watch, "it's almost ten o'clock and I've got a twelve mile ride to do. Seriously, Dan, if trouble starts between the sheepmen and cowmen, which side are you going to back?"

"Would you say, in the remote event of trouble, that a sheriff had ought to take sides in a range war?

"Shucks, there ain't no need for you to answer," he went on, without giving her the opportunity to do so even had she been so-minded. "There ain't going to be any range war. Just tell Cal Broughton that," he added with whimsical humor. "Just tell him I said that Judge Colt ain't goin' to be needed in Navajo County."

There was cold determination in the tone with which he uttered the last sentence.

Looking at him now, Dorinda recalled that Stuart had a reputation for being the sort of man who did whatever he set his hand to, and did it without regard for either hell or high water. Stubborn, some called him, though stubborn was not the term Cal Broughton's daughter would have used.

But even Dan Stuart's iron determination, she felt, would not be sufficient to keep trouble from the Cibecue this time. Things were coming to a head; there was the feel of war in the very winds that swept the Tonto Rim. But that Stuart would fight it, would strive to ward it off, she felt certain. There was a saying prevalent that it would be as easy to move Blue House Mountain as to swerve Stuart from any course he set his mind to.

"I'll tell Dad," she said, and added softly: "Don't forget you're always welcome at the Circle B."

After the girl's departure, Dan Stuart gathered up the papers on his desk and thrust them in a drawer. Deciding, this being payday night for most of the valley outfits, to take a final look round town before retiring, he picked up the black Stetson from the floor and left the scantily furnished office.

As he strode down the dusty street, its murky shadows dappled with golden bars of light streaming from open doors and windows, Stuart's thoughts turned to the troubled light he had observed in Dorinda's eyes.

Something was worrying her. Judging from her conversation it was the possibility of an open clash between the cowmen, headed by her father, and the sheepmen camped at Picture Rock, a few miles southwest of town. If *that* was her trouble, she need not burden her shoulders with it. His lips curved sardonically: He could name at least twenty ranchers in the county who were troubled by the same possibility.

The sheriff had not left the county seat at Holbrook through any special anxiety to view the scenery at the southern edge of his jurisdiction.

He tramped about for some time aimlessly, mulling over things in his mind. Abruptly, hearing his name called, Stuart looked up and found himself before the great frame structure that bore upon its false-fronted second story the legend:

BUCKET OF BLOOD SALOON

A man stood peering out at him from between the swinging doors. Shorty Glyman, a small rancher from the northern end of the valley, stout, bald-headed, a man who always wore a hat.

"Hey, Stuart!" he called. "Come on in here a minute. Some of the boys wants tuh palaver with yuh."

"It's kinda late," Stuart hinted. "I'm pretty tired, Glyman— I did a heap of ridin' today."

"A heap o' ridin'? Hell! I wish I had your job! Anyhow, it ain't more'n ten, or mebbe ten-thirty. Come on in awhile. 'Never turn in without waterin' the inner man' is a good motto in thirsty country like this here Cibecue."

Stuart grinned and climbed the steps to the resort's veranda. "I should think you'd be afraid of rusting your pipes drinking water. Thought I heard someone say you never downed anythin' less potent than *tequila*."

"Sho, now; by 'watering' I didn't mean *water!*" Glyman muttered.

The sheriff followed the bald-headed rancher inside the saloon. Several men whom Stuart knew were standing at the bar. From the rear of the long room came the whir of a wheel, the rattling of chips and a hum of low-voiced talk. Punchers spending their month's pay; staking it on the turn of a card, the frenzy of poker, the pause of a ball.

It was payday night. The town was full of cow-pokes; many of them were in this room, boys from the Flying Y, the Box T, the Twisted Arrow and the Circle B. It was their night to howl, and they aimed to do so as long as their money held out.

The men at the bar greeted Stuart. Ranchers, these, solid citizens of the county; men who had helped elect him. Men who knew him, trusted him, expected his support.

"What d'yuh know, Stuart?" said one, slapping him on the back. "D'yuh reckon there's gonna be trouble in the valley? Things are gettin' kinda ugly, I'd say."

"Yeah," said another. "I hear them sheepmen is aimin' tuh cross the Cibecue. What do yuh make of that, Dan? Sorta looks like they're spoilin' for trouble, eh?"

"Mighty lucky you happened along around here today, Stuart," growled Vic Tyrone, who owned the Flying Star. "I reckon we'll need your backin' 'fore this mess is over. If them mutton-eaters figgers tuh cross the Cibecue with their stinkin' bla-bla's, things is gonna end in gunsmoke. This is cowman's country; we don't want no sheep around here!"

Stuart looked the speaker over coolly. Vic Tyrone was a burly man with a trick of tilting his head a bit to one side when he talked or met another man's gaze. At some time during his life

15

he had evidently received a nasty wound, for there was a livid scar across his right temple, just below his hat brim. Tyrone had a reputation as a heavy drinker, and his looks at the moment did nothing to belie this repute. His little eyes were red-rimmed and sullen.

"Take it easy, boys. There won't be no range war," Stuart said quietly.

The men stared, one or two grinned faintly.

"Wal, I sure hope not," Shorty Glyman muttered, and taking off his hat, he mopped his glistening head with his neckerchief. After replacing his hat, he added:

"But us boys ain't aimin' to stand for no sheep around this valley, I'll tell yuh that, Sheriff."

"You're damn right we ain't!" Tyrone growled. "What I say is them mutton-eaters better step soft an' easy. We ain't lookin' for trouble—but we ain't runnin' from it, neither!"

"It's talk like you're making, Tyrone, that gets trouble started. If the sheepmen try to cross your range, let me know and I'll stop them. But if you go trying to take matters into your own hands—an' this goes for the rest of you fellows, too—watch out. There'll be no range war in this county if I can help it."

Vic Tyrone thrust his head to one side. "Feelin' kinda proddy since we voted you into the sheriff's office, ain't yuh?"

Stuart stared straight into Vic Tyrone's red-rimmed eyes. It was Tyrone's gaze that finally fell away.

"Yeah," Stuart's soft drawl was even. "I always feel kind of proddy when I hear your brand of chin-music."

A moment longer Stuart stared at the burly rancher. Then, with a curt nod to the others, he turned and left the resort.

As he was about to pass the dark alley running between the Bucket of Blood and the Warwhoop Hotel, the sheriff came to an abrupt pause.

For long seconds after hearing the startled cry, Dan Stuart stood there, to one side of the shadowy lane. Stood silent and peering. Stood bent forward, slightly crouching, each hand clamped round the smooth, worn butt of a leveled forty-five.

What was happening in that murky alley? Was some crime being committed there under cover of the night? Or, and more likely, was this not some sort of trap being cunningly baited for him by unknown enemies?

A groan, low and plaintive, drifted out from the impenetrable murk between the buildings.

The sheriff tensed, strained slowly forward, trying to cleave the shadows with staring eyes, trigger-fingers ready to squeeze cold steel. That groan, he told himself, sounded awful agonizing. Full of misery, sort of. But a fellow couldn't be sure, and it paid to be cautious around Cibecue now. Boot Hill housed plenty of gents whose impulse to action had once leaped beyond restraint.

He stood there motionless, narrowed eyes straining to pierce the murky shadows of that Stygian gloom. Then abruptly the silence of the night was torn by a ghastly rising gurgle that was like a rattle of breath in the throat of a dying man.

Relaxing slightly, Stuart grinned. "That fellow is a real actor," he thought, admiringly. "Clever the way he chokes it off in a sort of gasping wheeze. I reckon if I moved out of this shadow, it would be me that would be doin' the wheezing."

It was good enough to have fooled many men, he was thinking; then he caught sight of a stealthily moving shadow slinking off among the lesser shadows at the passage's far end, the end which gave upon the saloon's rear exit.

The following instant the night echoed to the running clump of the sheriff's boots as he went lunging forward through the dark curtain that shrouded the narrow space between the two buildings.

He paused, crouched motionless, listening.

But he could catch no sound save that of his own breathing. Holstering one of his weapons he struck a match. Revealed in its flickering light lay the out-sprawled figure of a man. He had fallen on his side. One arm was doubled under him, the other was outflung, much as it must have been when he was falling.

Cautiously, even yet more than half suspecting some sort of trap, the sheriff moved closer.

When he saw the man's face his eyes bulged, the gun sagged in his hand.

"Cal Broughton!" the name leapt to his startled lips.

He stood rigid, immobile as a man of stone, while his mind struggled to comprehend the meaning of this tragic death. Slowly he stooped and knelt beside the inert figure of Dorinda's father. The hilt of a knife stood out between the old cowman's shoulder blades. There was blood on the vest around it.

Grim of face, he got to his feet. The import of this crime, its possible consequences to Cibecue Valley and to himself and his position here, occurred to him at once. The flaring fires of hate which, up to now had smouldered, would soon burst in the flame of spitting guns.

Big Cal Broughton, hater of sheep, was dead!

2

The steady hum of voices coming from the Bucket of Blood Saloon was suddenly drowned in the crash of a pistol shot. Whining lead snuffed the sheriff's match. A livid spurt of flame from the shadows showed where the would-be assassin had stood.

Stuart swore, and flipped his weapon level. Flame belched from its muzzle as he sent a hail of lead searching through the shadows. His heart set up a wild pounding against his ribs as he went plunging forward in a crouching, zig-zag run.

He slowed to a stop at the far end of the dark alley and scanned the shadows with narrowed probing eyes. But he saw no further sign of the killer, and there came no sound of the man's departing footfalls.

Dan Stuart took a firm grip on himself; it was time for quick thinking.

He had left Holbrook with a single problem—that of nipping this threatened range war in the bud. His first act on arriving in Cibecue yesterday had been to visit the sheepmen's camp at Picture Rock, near Blue House Mountain. The result had been entirely unsatisfactory; a second problem confronted him. And now a third had been added to the list. And the third was bidding fair ultimately to become the most important of them all: who was this unknown killer, and would he be able to bring the man to justice?

There could be small doubt but that hell would pop when the cattlemen in town learned of Big Cal Broughton's killing. Plainly it was up to Stuart to conceal the crime as long as possible.

The sheriff was thumbing cartridges into the empty chambers of his pistol as he stood mulling things over. And though his thoughts were busy, his eyes also were keenly alert to catch the slightest suspicious movement or stirring of the shadows.

Why had Cal Broughton been murdered? The most obvious answer came instantly; Dan Stuart clenched his jaws.

There was something about the climate, the country, here in Arizona that got into a man's blood. Something that impressed upon a man the necessity for constant conflict. The pungent breath of violence was in the very atmosphere; in the stark buttes farflung across the country; in the towering rock escarpments of the dead and naked mountains; in the blistering sands of the arid wastelands with their whirling dust-devils and the gurgling yellow waters of their infrequent streams.

It was in the spined vegetation, too, and in the twisted thorny branches of the stunted trees. It was in the poisonous reptiles and insects of the land. It was in the desolation that brooded over these vast expanses of windswept range.

This was a hard country, and in it none but hard men could ever hope to endure.

The sheriff's thoughts were put to rout as the rear door of the Bucket of Blood banged open. Out poured a hoard of booted cowmen, intent on learning the cause of those sudden shots.

Stuart, in the light streaming out the open door, was quickly surrounded by the booted victims of overt curiosity. Sheathing his pistol, he scanned the eager, excited countenances, and his lean, square jaw clamped tight. These were cowmen; hasty, impulsive, hot-blooded men— men who would turn ugly at news of a cowman's death. They must not learn of Broughton's fate, not yet.

He forced a laugh. "Why the stampede, boys?"

"We heard shots!" growled one.

"What's up, Stuart?" demanded several others almost simultaneously.

"Shucks, you boys don't want to get all stirred up over some gent lettin' off a little steam," he chided gently. "He—"

"Hell, it sounded tuh me like a coupla rannies was doin' that shootin'!" Vic Tyrone growled, thrusting himself forward, a gaunt, rawboned man at his heels. "You tellin' the truth, Stuart?"

The sheriff looked Tyrone up and down. "Do you know any reason why I shouldn't be?"

A sudden quiet descended upon the ring of men that circled Stuart.

Tyrone licked his heavy lips, shifted his feet uneasily. He found it hard to meet the sheriff's level gaze.

The tall, rawboned man came abruptly to the burly rancher's support. Stepping to Tyrone's side, he stared at the sheriff insolently. "I reckon," he said, in a sneering tone, "you ain't above tellin' a lie when it suits your purpose."

Stuart, apparently, was unaffected by these doubts of his veracity. He turned to face the rawboned man and his eyes were still cool and level. His voice was quiet:

"Are you calling me a liar, Broughton?"

Jabe Broughton's gaunt, rawboned frame sagged forward in a crouch. His head thrust forward, like that of a snake about to strike. There were flecks of fire in his smouldering eyes, and his lips were drawn back from his yellowed teeth. He had run against Dan Stuart for sheriff in the recent election, and it seemed the sting of his defeat had not yet worn away.

"If the boot fits," he growled, "pull it on!"

Through vacuous eyes Stuart watched the thinning of the throng behind the speaker. There was a faint smile of contempt upon his lips. Hooking his thumbs in his gun belts in such a manner that his lean fingers lay close to the worn butts of his holstered .45s, he looked Jabe Broughton in the face.

"Might as well take the chip off your shoulder,

Jabe," he spoke slowly, as though weighing each word before releasing it. "The fellow who fired those shots has gone. If you think more than one man fired the shots you heard—why, that doesn't give us cause for a quarrel. This is a free country, I've heard. Every gent has a right to his own opinion."

Broughton stared in some amazement. "Takin' water, are yuh?"

"No, I ain't takin' water. You're tryin' to force a fight on me because I got elected sheriff and you didn't. I don't see no sense in slinging lead over a thing like that. The people made their choice."

Broughton's high-boned face went red. With a muttered oath he shouldered his way out of the circle and reentered the saloon, banging the door behind him.

Someone snickered.

"I reckon Jabe is a mite het up," a man said gravely. Several of his companions chuckled. "He's a hot-headed cuss," said another. "If it wa'n't for his ol' man, I cal'late Jabe would be on the warpath ag'in' them sheepmen right this minute. He's mighty much set ag'in' sheep."

But Stuart was not listening. He was staring over Vic Tyrone's left shoulder at a man who stood on the edge of a pool of light thrown from an unshaded rear window of the Bucket of Blood.

The man was a stranger, a dried-up wisp of a chap whose clothes hung from his bony limbs like the cast-off garments on a scarecrow. He was clad in range garb, and it was covered with powdery alkali dust as though from a long ride.

Stuart's curiosity was aroused. The advent of strangers was not a common occurence at Cibecue. There was little to entice strangers to the tiny hamlet beneath the Tonto's frowning rim. Who was this man, and why was he here? Why had he come at this particular time when the winds of trouble were blowing strong? Was there a sinister significance in his presence here tonight?

Seeing the sheriff's gaze upon him, the little man turned and slipped away among the shadows.

Stuart collected his scattered thoughts. "You was sayin', Vic?"

"I was sayin' that us fellas ain't aimin' to stand for no damn sheep in Cibecue Valley—"

"Oh, the old song," Stuart jibed. "It would go better if you could find some new words for it."

Since Broughton's slamming of the door, Tyrone's features were in shadow and the sheriff could make little of the burly rancher's expression. But his tone left little doubt as to what it was:

"Yeah? Well, I'm sayin' that we ain't gonna have no sheep round here. This is cow country an' it's gonna keep on bein' cow country! If them— Hell! a man's got a right to protect his property! The law says a man can fight to defend his property—"

25

"The law has been changed," Stuart drawled. "The first man that starts a fight with them sheepmen is goin' to jail, soon's I get my hands on him. The same thing applies to a sheepman who starts things with a cowman. You better keep that in mind, Tyrone, an' hogtie your mouth for a spell."

A low growl rose from several of the listeners.

"I'm kinda surprised at you, Stuart," said a bronzed, grim-lipped rancher beside him. "When I helped vote you into the sheriff's office, I figured you'd back us cowmen if it came to a fight with the wool-growers—"

"It ain't comin' to a fight, Blain. That's what I'm tryin' to make you fellas understand. If you'll keep your hands out of this business and leave things to the law, there won't be no chance for trouble in Cibecue Valley. The sheepmen know they can't get far buckin' the law. But when it comes to a scrap with cowmen, they usually decide to take a chance.

"Here's another thing to remember, Blain. The cowmen don't *always* win."

"If them sheepmen try to cross this valley we'll fight!" Blain snapped, and strode away, muttering to himself.

"Damn right we will," snarled Vic Tyrone, encouraged by this support. "An' when the smoke clears away, Stuart, them sheep-herdin' friends of yoren won't be nothin' more than a bad memory round these parts!"

"You've got no kick as long as they stay where they are," Stuart's tone was cold, vibrant with authority. "There's water an' feed enough around Picture Rock to last them a right considerable spell. Druce will use his head an' keep them there if you hombres show good sense and leave them alone."

"Hell!" Shorty Glyman piped up. "A lot you know about sheepmen. They're like sod-busters; they ain't never satisfied. The only way tuh keep 'em contented is tuh give 'em the earth with a picket fence around it!"

"Yeah," Tyrone concluded; "You mark my words, fella—let jest one of them blasted critters start across this valley for the Tonto Rim an' we'll wipe 'em up if the whole damn valley has tuh run blood!"

3

As Sheriff Dan Stuart headed for his office, his thoughts were far from idle.

What significance did the presence of the little alkali-covered stranger hold? Who was he? Where had he come from? Was Cibecue his destination, or was he en route for some more distant spot? What did he know about Big Cal Broughton's death?

Broughton's death! *That* was the big problem now! Who had killed Cal Broughton? And why had he been killed?

Broughton, the elder, was one of the pioneers of this country; a solid citizen, a wealthy rancher, a man whose word had carried weight.

Cal Broughton, whose open-handed generosity had never permitted him to drive a bargain wholly favorable to his own interests. Indian fighter, pioneer, cowman. Cal Broughton, who had never turned a hungry man from his door, be he cowpoke, range tramp, or outlaw. A man who had known cattle, horses, and hombres; who had stood four-square for law and order.

And now Cal Broughton lay cold and still in a dark alley, with a knife driven to the hilt in his back!

Someone should pay! Dan Stuart swore it.

The sheriff paused by the hitch rack before entering his lighted office. That light meant that his deputy, Nip Wingate, the man who normally kept law and order in Cibecue Valley, was still up. It meant more than that, but at the moment Stuart had eyes only for the two strange horses tied to the rail. One of them, a little blue roan, seemed vaguely familiar.

He racked his mind to think where previously he had seen it. And suddenly the answer came: The blue roan was Campero's old pack horse.

And Campero was boss herdsman for the Druce sheep outfit!

With a muttered oath, Dan Stuart mounted the wooden steps, strode into the lamp-lit office.

A man occupied the chair back of the sheriff's desk, sat tilted back against the unpapered wall. A man with an old pipe between his grim lips, and a scowl between his puckered eyes—Nip Wingate, Deputy Sheriff.

Wingate looked up at the sheriff's entrance, and the scowl between his eyes grew deeper.

Stuart's glance flashed here and there about the scantily-furnished office in probing stabs, came to rest upon the short, squat form of the man standing before the desk, his fingers nervously twirling the shabby sombrero he was holding in his hands.

The man was Campero. His faded eyes held a furtive gleam as they darted suspicious glances from the deputy to Stuart. His swarthy, saddle-leather face seemed not as dark as when Stuart had seen it yesterday at the camp by Picture Rock. And there was a large vein pulsing nervously on the sheepman's forehead.

Stuart's gaze left the Mexican and passed to the deputy's bunk along the farther wall. An inert figure lay upon it, the figure of a sleeping man. The figure of Druce, the sheepman.

With a sudden start the sheriff crossed the room in three long strides, stood looking down at Druce, the man who had dared bring sheep to the Cibecue. And, as he stared at the motionless form, Stuart's lips grew tight and thin. Druce was asleep, all right. But from his slumber there would be no awakening, for his was the sleep of Death.

The sheriff turned to the Mexican herder. "Hadn't you better tell us about this?"

Campero shrugged, ran his tongue across lips that did not moisten.

"See here, Campero," Stuart's tone was stern. "You'd better talk an' talk fast. What happened to Caspar Druce?"

Campero's little black eyes looked frantically about the room, like the eyes of a cornered animal seeking a means of escape. He seemed in the grip of an awful fear.

"Well?"

"I do not *sabe, señor*."

"What don't you understand?"

"I do not *sabe* how the patron met *el muerto*."

Nip Wingate removed his battered pipe to jeer: "That's what you greasers allus say!"

"It ees the truth, *señor.* Tonight w'en I return to the camp at Picture Rock, I fin' the patron on the ground outside hees tent. I'm look close an' *Sangre de Dios*! the patron ees dead!" Campero crossed himself fervently.

"Got any idea about what time this was?" Stuart asked thoughtfully.

"*Si.* Eet was jus' after dark, *señor.*"

"Well, get on with it," Wingate growled from around his battered pipe.

"Then I peeck the patron up an' put him on the *caballo* an' breeng heem here."

"How did you happen to return to the camp at Picture Rock?" asked Stuart. "I understood that you were over with the flock on Blue House Mountain."

"*Si*," Campero bobbed his shaggy head. "But I am come to Picture Rock to get the ordairs from the *Señor* Bruskell—"

"Who's he?"

"He—he ees the kin to *El Señor* Druce."

"Then how did you happen to go to Druce's tent?" Wingate snapped. "If it was dark you couldn't have seen him lyin' there."

Campero blinked. "I—I look—I see the light eenside the patron's tent, an' by the light I see the figure on the ground. Then—"

"Did you see Bruskell anywhere around?" Stuart asked.

"I stoop over the patron; then I'm hear the leetle sound like foot on twig. I'm look up queek an' see—"

Suddenly some glittering thing flashed in through the open window, striking the Mexican in the chest with a thump! As he went reeling backward, his voice choked off in a startled cry. He spun half around, staggered, swayed against the desk, his dark hands clawing at the knife-hilt which protruded from his breast above the heart.

Stuart and Wingate looked on in wide-eyed consternation, motionless with horror. For a long moment they stood as though frozen in their tracks, stunned by the suddenness, the sheer audacity of the thing. Then Stuart, swearing, leaped forward to catch the Mexican's swaying figure while Wingate, dragging at his gun, sprang toward the door.

Too late!

Thudding hoofbeats rose from the dusty street outside, drowning momentarily the distant sounds of revelry from the hilarious cowpokes who were still whooping it up at the Bucket of Blood. Then the thudding sound of the fleeing hoofs grew dim.

As Campero's knees, no longer able to support his weight, crumpled, Stuart eased the Mexican's limp form to the floor. The herdsman moaned, and his black eyes stared into the sheriff's. There was no fear in them now, only a great calmness.

"The pocket, *señor*," he whispered feebly. His lips were stiff and white, his words so faint as to be almost beyond interpretation. "Een the pocket—I . . . I found eet . . . beside the . . . patron's body."

A bloody froth crimsoned the pallid lips. The breath rattled in his throat. His shaggy head fell back and he was still.

Stuart straightened to his feet.

Here in this office lay the second and third victims of the unknown killer. The man had become a menace! Plainly he had killed Campero to keep the man from revealing something. What? What did the Mexican know that had necessitated the eternal sealing of his lips? What had he been about to say when the assassin's blade had buried itself in his breast?

What was behind these three wanton slayings, these ghastly murders in a single night? What was the secret the killer was trying to keep? Or was it but the start of the range war which had threatened the Cibecue ever since, a week ago, the sheepmen had appeared at Picture Rock?

Dan Stuart, newly-elected sheriff of Navajo County, did not know.

He ran a hand that was not quite steady through his rumpled yellow hair and sighed. "A good man, Campero."

Nip Wingate returned to the office. "The murderin' skunk got clear away. I never even caught a smell of him!"

"What color horse was he ridin'?"

"I couldn't even make that out, Dan. By the time I got outside an' to the bend in the street, his nag was jest a cloud of dust in the distance." The deputy puffed thoughtfully on his pipe for several moments. "So he killed the Mex, eh? Looked through his pockets, yet?"

There was an odd light in Stuart's eyes as they searched Nip Wingate's seamed and weather-bitten face. "Not yet." He was thinking that it was highly improbable that the deputy had heard Campero's last words if he had actually rushed to the street in an endeavor to sight the fleeing killer. "Do you know any particular reason why I ought to?"

Shoving back his hat, Wingate scratched his head. "Guess not. Only I expect it's sorta customary for the sheriff's office tuh go through the pockets of such corpses as comes to its attention. Leastways, that's allus been my experience."

"You've had considerable experience with sheriff's offices then, I take it?"

"Wal, I dunno—jest average, I reckon."

Stuart nodded. "I'll look through his pockets when I get around to it. I— Oh, howdy, Marshal."

Wingate's eyes flashed to the door. A man was

standing there, blinking in the lamp light as though he had just arrived. The man was Obe Shelty, of insignificant stature and a pair of tiny squinting eyes. He was Marshal of Cibecue, and no favorite of Deputy Wingate's.

"Hullo, Sheriff. Hope yuh didn't come clear down from the county seat jest on account of that two-bit range war folks is—"

"What range war?" Stuart's even voice cut through the marshal's piping, bullfrog squeak like a knife through butter. "What range war are you referrin' to? Tonto Basin? Pleasant Valley? Lincoln County?"

"Huh?" Obe Shelty blinked his squinting eyes. "Gosh, no!" he squeaked. "I'm talkin' about the one folks claims is headin' for Cibecue Valley!"

"What folks do you mean? Mention a few, Marshal. I'm right much interested—didn't have no idea there was trouble in the Cibecue."

"Why—why— Gosh a'mighty, Sheriff! Where'd yuh git them corpses?" Shelty's squinty eyes were suddenly big and round and staring.

"They jest walked in an' lay down where yuh see 'em, Obe," remarked Wingate, drawing a deep mouthful of smoke and blowing it at the cobwebbed ceiling. "Where did yuh think we got 'em?"

"Knifed!" ejaculated the marshal, as though making a discovery. "That—that one on the bunk is Druce, the sheepman, ain't it?"

"Right, as usual," Wingate nodded.

"Wal, fer gosh sakes, tell me what happened to 'em!"

"They was knifed," Nip Wingate answered.

The marshal glared at his tormentor. "You must spend a heap of your time, Mr. Wingate, thinkin' up them smart remarks. No wonder folks is gettin' stabbed right an' left. It's a wonder to me the Sheriff tolerates yuh." He turned to Stuart: "Who killed 'em?"

"We haven't found out yet. How about answering my question now?"

"What question was that?"

"You was saying that folks was predictin' a range war. I want to know what folks."

"Why—why—Vic Tyrone an' Jabe Broughton an' Shorty Glyman, to mention several of the most important."

"Who else?"

"Why, everybody says this valley's headin' smack fer trouble. But," Shelty puffed up his little chest importantly, "you needn't worry about it, Sheriff. I can take care of it all right," his grin was reassuring.

"I've no doubt but what you can. However," Stuart's tone was dry, "your help will not be necessary. There isn't going to be any range war in this valley. You've been misinformed. Your friends, Broughton, Tyrone an' Glyman, are just talking to feel their chins wag."

"Gosh, don't never think it, Sheriff. Them fellas is smart—smart as three whips. You jest watch: In two shakes of an old steer's horn this valley will be burnin' powder from end to end!"

Stuart stared at him.

"The first man I catch with a gun in his hand," he said softly, "is goin' to jail. What's more, he's goin' to stay there till I get good an' ready to let him out. Tell that to your friends when you see them."

Marshal Shelty's jaw sagged open. Plainly he was amazed at the sheriff's attitude. "You—you—, Say! Are you sidin' with them blasted sheepmen?" he demanded.

"I'm representin' the law, Shelty, as I think it should be represented. I'm not takin' sides. I'm workin' for peace an' prosperity, and any man that goes against that policy will find himself lined up against me."

"I expect you'll have a lot of high-powered enemies, then!" the marshal snapped, and turned. He was stopped at the door by Stuart's blunt: "Why?"

Shelty half turned to remark caustically:

"'Cause every cowman that's worth his salt will fight if sheep set foot in this valley!" and, wheeling angrily, he departed, slamming the door behind him.

Wingate grinned around his pipe. "That's talkin' turkey," he commented.

"Obe Shelty," Stuart said, "is a plain damned fool."

The deputy chuckled. "That's one thing you an' me can agree on!"

The sheriff stooped above Campero's motionless form. Carefully he commenced his search of the dead man's pockets. "Nip," his tone was sober, "there's a polecat loose on this range that stands in need of some gun medicine quick."

"Referrin', I reckon, to the knife specialist," Wingate opined, knocking the ashes from his pipe.

There was silence for a moment.

"Referrin' to the knife specialist. We've got to stop that hombre sudden or that range war everybody's shootin' off their mouths about will bust sure as hell." Stuart stared up into the deputy's wrinkled features. "What are we gonna do?"

"Wal," Wingate grinned, "we might set down an' keep tally for him."

Stuart grunted. "That's a hell of a joke at a time like this. Three killin's in one night is a heap sight too many! A whale of a sight too many when you take into account the importance of the victims!"

"I wouldn't consider a Mexican sheepherder of much importance," Wingate differed. "Nor a sheep owner like Druce, neither. Druce was nervy, bringin' sheep in here—I'll grant yuh that much. But I don't reckon none of the citizens here will do much weepin' on account of him gettin' rubbed out. They'd be a heap more likely to take up a donation tuh buy the killer a medal. You said three killin's—who's the third victim?"

"It's my notion that Druce was the first," said Stuart, going on with his search of the dead man's pockets. "Campero was the third. The second was—"

He broke off abruptly as his hand came out of the Mexican's right trousers pocket with a crumpled bit of cambric. It was the only alien thing he had so far uncovered, and there was little doubt in his mind but what this square of blue cloth that he was smoothing out upon his knee was the thing the dead man had referred to as being found beside Druce's body.

As he crouched there above the Mexican, staring at his find, Dan Stuart's lips straightened to a thin white line, tight-pinched at either corner.

It was a girl's handkerchief that lay spread upon his knee.

Stuart crushed it suddenly in a clenching fist. But if the movement had been designed to keep the bit of cambric from the deputy's staring gaze, it came too late.

"Cripes!" the battered pipe seemed in imminent danger of falling from Wingate's mouth. "Cripes! That belongs to Dorinda Broughton!"

4

The handkerchief of Cal Broughton's daughter found in the pocket of a sheepman! Nip Wingate was right; there could be little doubt that the bit of cambric was Dorinda's property. For a ranch girl, she was not only original but particular about her kerchiefs. They must be cambric, and they must be blue. And the one in Stuart's fist was both.

How did it happen to be found beside the dead body of Caspar Druce, the murdered sheepman? Assuming that it had not been, and that Campero's story was false, how did it come to be in the Mexican's pocket? To be sure, he could have found it, but that explanation rang a little flat in Stuart's ears.

He was, he told himself, much more easily persuaded that the bit of cambric had actually been found by Campero, and found beside Druce's body. God knew it was bad enough even that way—with her father lying dead and cold in the dark alley that ran between the Warwhoop Hotel and the frame structure housing the Bucket of Blood Saloon.

Not that he doubted her. It was of what other folks would think, and possibly say when they heard the story, that Dan Stuart was pondering.

The thing was fantastic, impossible! Dorinda, no matter what impelling motives urged her on, would never go alone at night to the camp of a sheepman!

But wouldn't she? In perfect frankness, he was forced to admit that he could conceive of circumstances under which she would. She was a sensible girl—the whole valley said so. But she was courageous, too. She would, he knew, do what she believed to be the right thing, regardless of the consequences. When it came to Right and Wrong, she knew no compromise.

After all, perhaps she had not gone alone. Perhaps her father had gone with her, or she with him. It was a comforting thought; but strangely, Stuart was not comforted.

The sheriff of Navajo County was more worried and puzzled than he would have cared to admit.

Who was the silent, slinking killer who had snuffed three lives in a single night? It was like an owl's refrain, that insidious who—who—who?

Who had killed Caspar Druce beside his tent in the camp at Picture Rock? And why had the man found it necessary to kill Druce? What had the sheepman done, or known, or suspected that had made his life a menace to the unknown assassin of Cibecue?

Had Dorinda been at the sheepman's camp when the man from New Mexico was being killed? If so, had she seen his murderer? And if she *had* seen him, would she be able to identify him if she saw him again?

Dan Stuart thought not. Such largess was far in excess of that which the gods in their wisdom thought fit to bestow on mortal man.

"Ah!" Abruptly the sheriff thought he saw a more probable reason for the worried light he had detected in the eyes of Dorinda Broughton earlier in the evening. Her worry, he now believed, had had nothing to do with the possibility of a range war in Cibecue Valley. She had been dreading discovery of her visit to the sheepman's camp!

Lord, was this still the same night she had paid him that fleeting visit? He glanced at his watch and found that it still lacked well over an hour till daylight. Plainly it was the same night—and yet it seemed incredible that so many things could have been crowded into the small space of a single dozen hours!

Who had killed Cal Broughton, that upright, foursquare man who, during his life, had bossed the cowmen of Cibecue Valley? And why had *he* been killed? Surely it was beyond the bounds of reason to believe that he and Caspar Druce had shared a secret! Equally hard did the sheriff feel it to believe that he and Druce together had done something which had merited their sudden deaths.

Stuart could conceive of no circumstances under which Cal Broughton, hater of sheep and sheepmen, could have played the role of partner to Caspar Druce.

What, then, lay behind these sudden slayings? What was the hidden key to these ghastly crimes, and where should he seek it? Or was this but the work of some wandering maniac?

No; the thing went deeper, showed crafty planning and ruthless execution! Perhaps, after all, this was the beginning of the heralded range war.

Campero's death, he felt, could not be placed in the same category with the deaths of Broughton and Druce. Campero had undeniably been killed to seal his mouth. What was the revelation he had been about to make when that eight-inch blade came slithering through the open window?

Question after question ploughed its dreary furrow across young Stuart's mind. But the answers all eluded him. An exasperated grimace crossed his bronzed features, and the corded muscles stood out rope-like on his jaw. What a damnable, inexplicable mess this seemed to be. A devil's brew and no mistake!

He turned to his deputy.

"Was Campero here very long before I came?"

"Campero?" Wingate completed his task of pressing fresh tobacco into the bowl of his blackened pipe. "Wal, around half an hour, I expect. He wa'n't very responsive-like tuh questions, though, till you started in on him. All

I'd been able tuh get out of him was 'No *sabe*,'—them cussed greasers is all alike."

Stuart commenced pacing restlessly up and down the narrow room, chin on chest, brooding eyes unseeing. Puffing thoughtfully, Nip Wingate watched him. The clock on the sheriff's desk ticked loudly in the silence. Of course there were other sounds: that of the sheriff's booted feet as he tramped up and down, up and down, up and down; the sound of the rising wind in the night outside, and the creak of the sheriff's gun belts as he moved. But that was all.

Nip Wingate studied the smoke from his pipe as it spiralled and swirled, floated and eddied and drifted about the cobwebbed ceiling.

The sheriff stopped before his desk, looked down at Wingate where he sat tilted back against the wall behind it.

"Nip," he said slowly, "Cal Broughton was murdered tonight in that little alley that runs between the Bucket of Blood and the Warwhoop. He's lyin' out there now with a knife in his back."

"Cripes! Cal Broughton! Wal, I swan!" the deputy's eyes had narrowed till the puckered skin of his lids almost hid them from the sheriff's gaze. "So," he mused softly, "Cal Broughton was the second victim of our mysterious knifeman."

Grim-lipped, the sheriff nodded. He supplied the details, so far as he knew them. Mentioned his brush with Tyrone, and the man's belligerent attitude.

"Yeah, that fella's *el hombre malo*, an' no mistake," the deputy promptly agreed. "He's got a itch tuh carve himself out some more territory—he's got ambition, Tyrone has. He's the sort of gent a fella would be well-advised tuh keep his eyes on. What I mean, *all* the time."

He puffed thoughtfully for several moments, blowing little smoke rings toward the ceiling. "But as fer Broughton—wal, I been sort of expectin' . . ." His voice trailed off to silence.

Stuart's glance was sharp. "Been expectin' what?"

"Wal, jest let it go like that. I been expectin'," Wingate said. "There ain't no sense in suspectin' Campero of polishing Cal off, howsomever. A fella might take a notion to suspect the Mex of killin' Cal as revenge for Druce's death. But Campero couldn't of done it even if he'd been thinkin' of it, an' thought Broughton had had a hand in his boss' finish."

"How so?"

"Because, at the time Cal Broughton was bein' stabbed, accordin' to your own timin', the Mex was standin' right here in this office refusin' tuh answer my questions about Druce."

Stuart resumed his tramping up and down the room. And once again a brooding hush descended on the office of the sheriff at Cibecue.

All trails, he thought ironically, returned to that one all-absorbing question: "Who was the killer of Cibecue?" And in comparison, the problem of a possible range war shrank away to insignificance.

What was the deadly secret the man was striving to keep? How could it involve both Druce and Broughton, heads of opposite factions? How came Dorinda to be tangled in this web of Satan's weaving? Was the killer's bloody trail run out, or was more gore to be spattered in his wake?

It was apparent to the sheriff that he could be forgiven should he fail to stop the range war. But it was startlingly plain that he would be held strictly accountable should he fail to apprehend the man or men behind these cold-blooded homicides. Somehow, he must find the solution, singular or plural, to these killings, and put the murderer, or murderers, behind the bars to await a jury's verdict and a judge's pronouncement of sentence.

It was a man-sized task!

Looking at his deputy, Stuart felt that Wingate's thoughts were following the pattern of his own.

The front legs of the deputy's chair hit the floor with a thud, and he got to his feet. "What's the first step on the program, Dan?"

The sheriff ran a hand through his curly rumpled hair. "What was Cal Broughton doin' in town tonight, Nip? Ain't got any ideas on the subject, have you?"

"Wal, it's payday night, or was—it's pretty dang near mornin' now, I reckon."

"That's so. I'd forgotten. He probably came in with some of his boys."

"If it comes to that," said Wingate conversationally, "what was Vic Tyrone an' Glyman doin' in town? An' Blain? An' Jabe Broughton? An' Miss Dorinda? I reckon they was all here fer the same reason. Payday night draws 'em all tuh the wheels o' Chance."

The deputy's words drove Stuart's thoughts back to Dorinda. She must have come to him straight from the camp at Picture Rock. No wonder there had been a troubled light in her fine blue eyes! Had she done no more than get a glimpse at the sheepman's outsprawled form, it surely would be more than sufficient explanation of her uneasy appearance.

Perhaps, he thought, she had missed her kerchief and had been wondering if by some unlucky chance it had fallen near Picture Rock. His heart went out to her. She was a spunky girl—most girls in her place would have been distraught, if not downright hysterical, after such an experience as she must have undergone.

Again the deputy's voice broke in upon his thoughts:

"Wal, what are we gonna do, Dan? We got tuh find that killer, all right; you smacked the nail on the head when yuh said that. An' if we don't work fast, before these cowmen find out about Broughton's massacree, there'll be guns a-spittin' all over this here valley. What do yuh want me tuh do?"

Stuart sighed. This was an aging business, and no doubt about it!

"Better go over an' see if you can wake up Allen," he said. "You an' him can take Broughton's body to the undertakin' parlors an' then come over here an' remove Druce an' Campero to the same place."

Allen was the coroner who, fortunately, was here at this time on a visit to his brother, who ran the General Store.

Wingate nodded, knocked the ashes from his pipe, and started for the door.

"By the way," Stuart added: "You'd better have Allen try and determine when these three fellows were killed. I want to be sure which was killed first. It may be important."

"I'll tell him, Dan."

Wingate tucked his pipe in his shirt pocket and opened the door. "Wal!" he muttered, and "Wal, come right in, Mister Tyrone. Don't be bashful. I reckon you know the sheriff, so there ain't no need for you tuh hang back that-away. Come right in."

As Wingate stepped aside to permit the burly rancher to enter the office, through Stuart's mind ran the thought:

What is Tyrone doing outside that door?

5

Inside the Bucket of Blood Saloon there were still six or eight men intent on disturbing honest men's slumber. These six or eight were booted, belted and spurred; cowmen, to a man. Tyrone was there, and Broughton. The dusty stranger in the too-large clothes was there, also. The rest were cowpokes from the valley outfits, several of whom were obviously under the weather. One misguided soul lay under a table.

Vic Tyrone was growling woe to an interested audience before the bar. "We was a bunch of damn fools fer votin' him into the Sheriff's Office!" he declared, smacking the bar with a heavy fist. "That's it—a bunch of knot-heads! Why, it's gettin' so he thinks he owns this blasted country. Tellin' us what we can do an' what we can't like he was a king or somethin'. I tell yuh I'm fed up!"

The little stranger was studying Tyrone with an air of cool appraisement. A tall burly man with hamlike hands, red hair and defiant, cynical red-rimmed eyes, Tyrone nevertheless was possessed of a magnetic personality. The livid scar across his right temple gave him a rakish, reckless air that was not always upheld by his actions. He had very likely seen a deal of life, and in some measure there must have been embodied in him the ingredients of leadership, for he was seldom unable to gather about him at least a handful of listeners.

Tyrone was leaning against the bar as he talked. Many of the cowpokes gathered about him were hanging eagerly on his every word, grinning Chessycat fashion whenever he said something that pleased them. One or two faces wore frowns. One appeared indifferent to his rantings; the face of the dusty stranger. No expression could be detected on his nondescript features. A gun belt sagged about his bony frame, and one long-fingered hand always seemed close to the butt of the heavy six-shooter that protruded from its scarred holster.

"So am I gettin' fed up on his high-an'-mighty ways!" Jabe Broughton spat. "Why Obe Shelty, the marshal, would of made a better sheriff tuh my way of thinkin'. What's things comin' to in this country when the sheriff can slap honest citizens in jail for defendin' their property! I tell yuh it's an outrage; he dassent do it! He's bluffin'! I vote we shoot hell outa them damned wool-growers!"

Two or three of the listening punchers seconded the motion.

"By Gawd," Broughton went on, his lips writhing back from his yellowed teeth as he warmed up to his subject, "we'll make her a corpse an' cartridge occasion for them blasted wool-growers if I got anythin' tuh say about it! They're figgerin' tuh take their blattin' ba-ba's across the Cibecue an' over the Rim. They'll have tuh use the ol' trail southeast of town tuh get 'em there. I say we ought tuh hole up along there someplace an' blast hell outa them!"

Tyrone's lips curled contemptuously. "An' *I* say you're goin' off haff-cocked as usual." Thrusting his head to one side, he regarded his audience with the grin of an amused wolf.

"What *I* say is, a blood-stampede will do the work. It'll do the work better'n we could ever hope tuh do with gun-play—an' his Blasted Majesty, King Stuart, won't be able tuh pin a damn thing on us!"

Admiration stamped the eager countenances of his listeners—most of them, that is. There were one or two faces in which admiration was lacking; that of the little stranger and one of Blain's punchers. The little man's countenance remained indifferent. The puncher seemed dubious.

"It sounds all right," he said, "I'll grant yuh that. But what about Stuart? He seems some set to prevent trouble in the Cibecue. An' I expect I ain't much anxious to cross a man like him. He's dangerous—cool an' dangerous."

Tyrone scowled. Broughton sneered. "Developin' a case of cold feet, eh? Better not let Blain catch yuh makin' such remarks."

The puncher flushed. "If I'm afraid to go against

Stuart, I reckon I'm not alone in my failin'. Dan Stuart's right smart of a man."

"Yeah," a second puncher spoke up. "He may be slow to anger, but he's hell on wheels when he gets started."

"I expect I been wrong in thinkin' this was a he-man's country," said Tyrone, with his head on one side. As he noted the puncher's blanching face his red-rimmed eyes took on a wanton, jeering gleam. "We got a bunch of two-legged panty-waists an' pussy-kitten squirts forkin' leather in the Cibecue, seems like."

The two punchers who had passed remarks anent Stuart began backing away from the look in Tyrone's eyes. Their hands went level with their shoulders to prove their peaceable intentions as they edged toward the door at the rear of the resort. Two or three of their former companions laughed, but made no overt moves. The punchers reached the door, pulled it open and hastily departed.

Broughton sneered. "You called the turn, Vic. We don't need no help from yeller-bellied skunks like them two. Let 'em go, an' good riddance."

A faint smile wreathed the stranger's lips as, turning his back, he ordered a drink.

Tyrone left the saloon.

As Vic Tyrone stepped into the Sheriff's Office, across his shoulder Stuart saw the blurred outline of a shadowy figure lounging against the corral across the street. Then his attention centered on the burly rancher confronting him. There was a dark scowl on Tyrone's face.

"I don't like that remark," he said.

"I didn't expect you would," Wingate told him equably, his hand on the butt of his holstered six-gun. "I didn't say it tuh compliment yuh."

"What were you doing outside that door, Vic?" Stuart asked quietly.

"What did yuh think I was doin'? Dustin' the steps? Hell! I was aimin' to come in, of course. Jest as I reached for the knob, ol' Sour Puss here pulled it open. Why? Is visitin' the Sheriff's Office agin' the law?" there was a jeering light in Tyrone's red-rimmed gaze.

Stuart looked the rancher in the eyes. His face was without expression, like a mask. Tyrone stood rigid, narrow-eyed, silent. His right hand was hooked by the thumb to his gun belt. The scar stood out white upon his forehead.

"No, Vic, I don't expect there is any law prohibiting a man from visiting a sheriff's office," Stuart's tone was low, cold and even. "But there's other things. Listening at keyholes is a mighty dangerous pastime."

The air in the scantily-furnished office became suddenly chilled and rarified. In the abrupt silence the clock on the sheriff's desk banged off the seconds with a sound not unlike that of a hammer beating on an anvil. No one moved. It was strange how still they stood.

Then abruptly Tyrone cursed.

"One of these days you'll go too damn far with your fresh talk," he blustered, red of face. "When that time comes you an' me, Dan Stuart, will go tuh burnin' powder!"

"I expect right now is about as good a time as any, Vic," a cold calm marked Stuart's voice.

Tyrone's muscles leaped and stiffened. The color drained from his face and Wingate could see that the rancher was suddenly awed and afraid. His widening gaze remained fixed on Stuart's face as though he dared not look away, and there were tiny beads of moisture on his forehead.

"I—I—" he swallowed nervously. "I ain't got time right now. I—I got to go," and he began backing slowly toward the door.

The sheriff's face was like a mask, so cold and calm it seemed. "Just as you say, Vic. If you ain't in *too* much of a hurry, though, I'd like to ask you a question or two before you leave."

Tyrone stopped his backing movement reluctantly. "What—what is it you're wantin' tuh ask me?"

The sheriff flicked a hand toward the figures that were occupying the bunks along the wall, the uncovered forms of Druce and Campero. "I don't expect you know how these men happened to get killed, do you?"

Tyrone started. Evidently he had not noticed the dead men until now. His white face went a trifle whiter. "My Gawd, no!" he muttered, and drew a shaky hand across his forehead. "What—how— Where did yuh find them?"

"Campero found Druce and brought him in. He was lying dead before his tent at the sheep camp by Picture Rock. Campero died in this office not much more than an hour ago."

Tyrone's stare was uneasy. He kept swallowing painfully, as though some alien substance had found lodgment in his throat. "Who . . . who did it?" he asked slowly.

"That's what I'm askin' you, Vic."

"You're askin' me?" the rancher echoed. "By Gawd, you got yore guts!"

Tyrone seemed to have regained some of his former composure. Tilting his head to one side, he sneered:

"You can't lay them murders at my door, Stuart. I ain't playin' goat for nobody!"

Flecks of fire appeared in Stuart's accusing eyes and fused: "Who said anything about murders, Vic Tyrone? Damn you, how did you know those men were murdered?"

Tyrone stepped backward like a man slapped suddenly across the face.

"I—" he grinned fatuously. "I inferred they'd been murdered from yore talk. I—" Then, furious, he swore. "You go tuh hell, Dan Stuart! I'm answerin' no more of yore damned framed-up questions!" He strode out the door with savage, clumping steps, not bothering to close it after him. A moment later the darkness had swallowed him up.

Stuart and Wingate were left alone.

6

Deputy Nip Wingate looked proud as a cat with kittens.

"Gosh, Dan," he muttered admiringly, "you sure made that polecat take water fast. He backed u so quick I thought he was goin' to step right smack on his tail! Whew! I'll bet he's mad enough tuh chew cold steel an' swaller it!"

Stuart was paying no attention. He was staring out the open door toward the corral across the road. The shadowy figure he had seen when Tyrone had entered the office a few minutes ago, now was gone. The mysterious stranger, if he it was, had vanished.

Wingate's face abruptly sobered as Stuart closed the door and sank to a seat behind his desk. He made as though to speak, closed his mouth, then opened it again:

"You want to keep yore eyes peeled for Vic, hereafter, Dan. He won't be forgettin' the way you made him take water. An' he won't forget that you come right close to accusin' him of those murders, neither. He can hate like an Injun, Tyrone can."

"That's his privilege," said Stuart coldly. "Do you think Vic had a hand in them killin's? You saw the way he acted when I tripped him up?"

"Yeah," Wingate got out his pipe and began to

whittle some tobacco from his plug of Brown's Mule. "I saw how he took it. But I don't know as he's got anything to do with them murders or not. He hates sheepmen, all right. An' I guess he'd jest as soon shoot 'em as look at 'em."

He put the plug and his knife away and pressed the tobacco chips into the blackened bowl of his pipe. "But I ain't never heard of Vic Tyrone usin' a blade on anybody."

"Then you don't reckon he had anything to throw dust for, eh?"

"Wal, I don't know as I'd go that far," the deputy declared, lighting his pipe. "There's mebbe a lot of things he's done that he wouldn't want made public. But I don't hardly think he's got any knifings to hide. Vic Tyrone is a gun-slinger, Dan. He ain't got much use for a knife. Knives come more natural to sheepherders—Mexes an' Basques. Leastways, that's allus been my experience."

"Uh-huh," Stuart nodded absently. Plainly, his thoughts had already left Tyrone. "Guess you'd better be gettin' over to Allen's, Nip. It's gettin' close tuh dawn. Tell Allen I said he's to check up on the time of these deaths; I want to know what order these fellows were killed in. It might be important."

Wingate nodded and slouched from the office, puffing smoke at every step.

When the deputy had gone, Stuart sat for some

time deep in thought. Finally he arose and pulled down the curtains on the two office windows. Going to the door, he opened it and stood staring toward the corral, which now he could not see due to the darkness being always heaviest just before the dawn.

He stood there for several moments, lost in meditation. Just as he was about to turn away and close the door, the sharp report of a rifle banged out from the direction of the pole corral. Glass tinkled and something clattered as, ducking, Stuart slammed the door.

His eyes were narrowed as he gave a swift glance about the lamplit room. The bullet of the unknown sniper had struck the clock on his desk, smashed it beyond repair. Stuart's lips tightened slightly as he thought how close he'd been to death.

He longed to go outside, to prowl for a sign of the would-be assassin, but knew that to open that door again immediately would be to invite destruction. There was every chance that the unknown bushwhacker had fled. But, he reminded himself sternly, it paid to be cautious in Cibecue. There was no harm in giving the killer a little more rope; he'd get him in the end. The thought was both a promise and a threat.

Stuart felt sure that the man who had just attempted to kill him as he stood there framed against the lighted office, was the unknown killer whose tally was three scalps in a single night.

Unseeingly he stood staring down at the battered clock upon the floor. His tousled yellow curls gave his grave features an engaging look. He was picturesque in his soft-topped range boots, his faded Levi's, blue flannel shirt and open pinto vest. He was picturesque, but would have resented it had anyone been frank enough to tell him so.

His narrow escape from death had apparently left him as unmoved as Tyrone's curses. The only sign of emotion he had shown, or now exhibited, was that slight tightening of the lips. Indeed, he seemed already to have forgotten the incident.

He appeared to be brooding, meditating over some involved, perplexing problem. That it was unconnected with the recent shooting was proved when, with a faint half smile, he produced Dorinda's handkerchief and stood regarding it with somber eyes.

After several moments, having apparently come to some decision, he drew a match from his pocket and, snapping the bit of wood to flame, held it beneath one corner of the crumpled cambric.

When the flame scorched his fingers, he dropped the tiny fragment that still remained unburned. When even that was reduced to fragile ash he placed his boot upon it, grinding it into the scarred wooden floor.

He realized that what he had done was wrong. But apparently it caused him no perturbation for his features remained unruffled, calm, cold, emotionless as ever.

As long as he kept silent, who could prove that he had ever taken a crumpled square of blue cambric from the pocket of a sheepman? Who, indeed?

The sheriff smiled.

He thought of how he had wooed Dorinda. It had been sudden, unexpected, her surrender to him. He had not thought it would be that way; he had more than half suspected that he would need undergo a long siege of her affections before, if ever, she yielded.

But it hadn't been that way. They had been talking together while riding home from a short visit to a nester family the girl had been secretly helping. They had stopped to rest their horses and suddenly he had found her in his arms. She was sweet. He was the luckiest man in the county, he told himself, as he had dozens of times before. He was not worthy of her, of course; but neither was any man, he felt.

He could see her smiling face as though she were standing before him now. He loved to watch the changing lights in her clear blue eyes, serene and calm as forest pools at noonday; and the rose blush in her satiny, sun-kissed cheeks; and the blue sheen in her intense black hair where the sunlight touched upon it. When he thought of her as she'd lain in his arms that day, a week ago tomorrow, he was hard put to control the trembling of his body.

There was a deal of spirit in the tilt of her chin; she was like old Cal had been—independent and courageous, with a mind of her own and the sense to use it. A girl in a hundred, he told himself, and thanked the gods she had consented to be his.

Abruptly the soft, reflective light in the sheriff's agate eyes gave way to their accustomed hardness. His figure grew rigid, and the tiny muscles stood out along his jaw. He had heard no sound, had seen no faintest movement, light, or shadow; yet abruptly he knew that he was not alone. Some sixth sense that is acquired by riders of the wastelands, warned him that staring eyes were fixed upon his back.

Slowly he turned around.

There in the open doorway, framed against the false dawn, stood a stranger. And the stranger's hand was curled round the hickory butt of a leveled forty-five. His rough voice emerged from about the stump of a black cigar that was clamped between his lips:

"Easy does it, Sheriff!"

7

The ranch headquarters of the Circle B was situated in a wide clearing ringed with quaking aspens. As Dorinda Broughton rode through the trees, she saw through the drooping, fluid foliage of a single giant pepper tree the moonlight slanting down upon the low, earth-roofed ranch house. There were no lights visible through its darkened windows. And she saw no pipe-glow on the wide veranda indicating that her father sat there. Indeed the place seemed deserted.

But there was a light in the foreman's shanty across the clearing, so she turned her horse in that direction. Hardly had she reached it as the door opened and Blinky Evans stood there regarding her in the light streaming out through the opening.

"I want to have a talk with you, Blinky. Has Dad returned from Cibecue?"

"I reckon not, ma'am. I ain't heard him."

"Is Jabe here?"

"No, ma'am. I ain't seen nothin' of yore brother either. Not since he rode outa here right after grub. It was just a few minutes 'fore you left, yoreself, ma'am."

Dorinda appeared to be thinking. "All right," she said, wearily. "Come over to the house in half an hour. I'll see you in the living room."

Dorinda clucked to her horse and moved toward the pole corrals that spanned the little creek. Stripping the gear from her animal, she turned him into the nearest enclosure, put up the pole bars, hung saddle and bridle over the topmost and turned toward the house, the spurs jingling on her booted feet.

The living room of the Circle B ranch house was long, low-ceilinged and cool. In the center of its long inner wall was a great fireplace of curly quartz. There were tables from Old Mexico and hand-hewn chairs with cowhide backs and seats.

Dorinda drew off her gloves and removed her hat. For several moments she walked aimlessly about the room, looking at the various ornaments upon its walls. The oak-framed Remingtons; the two border rifles hung above the fireplace; the mountain lion masks, and elk, and bear. She thought it odd that neither her father nor Jabe had yet returned from town.

Then, for a time, her thoughts turned to the man whom last week she had promised to marry— young Dan Stuart, the sheriff. Romantic looking, she thought him, with his black Stetson hat, his blue flannel shirts, his faded Levi's and soft-topped range boots with their glittering spurs. She liked the tousled way he wore his curly yellow hair. And she liked his eyes, their cold steadiness and serenity. And his lean-waisted manly figure.

She liked his close-mouthed reticence; he was a man who lived under his hat, as the cowboys said. Though sometimes his silences were exasperating, his calmness an irritation. She liked his pleasant drawl, his marvelous control of temper. He was a man whose conquest would thrill a good many women.

Yet there were times when she wondered. Why, for instance, was he so set on preventing a clash between sheep and cattle interests? Such things had happened elsewhere under other sheriffs and she had heard no complaints about their failing to prevent them. Such things were usually affairs which no one man could hope to stop. Yet Dan Stuart was plainly striving to avert an open clash in the Cibecue. Why? And why had he refused to say which side he would take in case of trouble?

He was a cowman, or had been until the people had elected him sheriff a few months ago and he had offered his ranch, the S Bar 4, for sale. A New Mexican firm had purchased; an organization known as the Tucumcari Pool. Their secretary, a man named Hoskins, had come on immediately and taken charge. Most of the old hands had been dismissed, the bulk of the cattle sold. The buildings, she understood, were being remodeled. There was a deal of speculation going on in the cow camps about the pool; speculation concerning the breed of cattle they would run, and about the size of the coming herds. About the men, too, and whether they would make good neighbors.

There was the clump of booted feet crossing the wide veranda, and a moment later Blinky Evans came striding in. He was middle aged, with pale watery blue eyes that were eternally blinky giving him his cognomen. His shabby Stetson was in his hands and when she told him to draw up a chair, he deposited it on the floor nearby.

"You was wantin' to see me, ma'am?"

"Yes. Do you know of any reason why Dad shouldn't be home by now?"

"Wal, I reckon. He told me when he left that he was figgerin' tuh spend the night in town, ma'am."

"Oh." Dorinda changed the subject. "What do you think of the sheriff, Blinky?"

"Dan Stuart?" the foreman blinked. "Why, I'd say that Stuart was pretty much of a man, Miz Dorinda, ma'am. A bit set in his ways, mebbe, but he's a fella a man could ride the river with. Lives under his hat, Dan does. To my way o' thinkin', ma'am, it would be a heap better if some other gents I could name would do the same."

Dorinda felt she knew one of the "gents" to whom Evans was referring. He had never cared very much for Jabe, she recalled.

The foreman, too, was doing a bit of thinking. He was thinking she looked worried. Her face seemed no paler than was its wont, but there was a troubled light in her fine blue eyes that Evans felt had no place there. He wondered what could be troubling her. Finally he ventured to ask.

Dorinda laughed. "Why, there's nothing troubling me, Blinky," she denied, but her laughter seemed a trifle forced.

"Wal, I reckon you know yore own mind, ma'am. But if there's any way I can be of help, don't hesitate tuh call on me. I reckon you know I think a heap o' you, Miz Dorinda, ma'am."

"Sure, I know you do, Blinky. And you know I think a lot of you, too. But there isn't anything bothering me, to speak of," she replied with a brave little smile.

When the foreman had gone, Dorinda put on a heavy sweater as protection against the coldness of the night and adjourned to the veranda where she seated herself in a comfortable rocker. Arizona nights grow cold once the sun has set, and a penetrating chill pervades the desert places. And so it was this night, but the moon was lovely.

The far reaches of the vast country lay bathed in an argent glow, shimmering, drowsing, peaceful. Close at hand the terrain dropped away in a sea of rounded contours. To the north were foothills, rising slopes that stretched hungrily to the Tonto Rim, dark with splotches of spruce, juniper, and above them all, the pines in their towering grandeur.

The veranda where Dorinda sat was a black void

of silence, lending itself admirably as a curtain for mental pictures and dreams and a young girl's romantic fancies. But Dorinda's eyes for a time were fixed on the far distances where the moon played on rocky ridge and bold escarpment. It was some time before she permitted herself to become lost in thoughts.

In the morning the outfit would all roll out before daybreak with a smell of frying bacon and boiling coffee in their nostrils, and in their ears the clatter of cooky's ladle on a wash-pan and his strident voice bellowing: "Roll out, yuh lazy sons! Roll out an' come an' get it or I'll throw it plumb away!"

Fully-dressed figures would then come tumbling from the bunkhouse, stamping their feet into range boots as they blinked the sleep from their eyes. Then the youngest waddy would swallow his beans and bacon whole and take the lining off his throat with scalding coffee that everyone knew was strong enough to kill an ox, and vanish into the violet haze of the approaching dawn with hopes of rounding up the cavvy.

With the horse herd turned into the pole corrals, would come a creaking of leather, a jingling of spur rowels, the flapping *swish* of chaps and the voices of flying ropes as the boys snaked out their mounts and saddled them with chattering teeth. Then off they'd go for their miles and miles of riding.

She envied them, tonight, and wished she, too, might have been born a man.

But then abruptly her thoughts returned to Stuart. As the silent moments passed her expression became more and more forbidding. Laughing Dorinda Broughton was not laughing tonight. The murky shadows on the veranda hid the worried light that had returned to her eyes, concealed the grimness of tight-pinched lips and furrowed brow.

A premonition seemed to have her in its grip; she was oppressed with a feeling of disaster. Something was wrong, she felt.

She tried to banish the morbid mood by thinking again of Dan Stuart. She told herself that she was in love with him, but somehow her heart remained unconvinced. Love, she thought, was a sense of complete trust, respect, adoration, unity. She could not honestly say she did not trust Dan, for she did trust him; too, she respected him above all other men, save possibly her father; she adored him. But she was not one with him.

Perhaps that was because he unthinkingly gave her so little of his confidence; kept himself so closely to himself. She could never guess his thoughts, seldom read his mind. He seemed to live aloof from people in a world that was entirely his own. He was too self-sufficient, she thought, or perchance a bit too self-centered.

He was always confident, capable, commanding;

a master of every situation. He seemed habitually wrapped in a mantle of impenetrable calm; his quiet efficiency was often cause for exasperation in a girl of Dorinda's temperament. She had a mind of her own and took no pleasure in having her lover solve all her problems for her in the confident, deliberate manner that was Dan Stuart's.

Too, that overpowering strength of character, which was undoubtedly his greatest possession, when coupled with that unswerving determination to have his way, to do whatever he attempted, was a side of his nature that always brought her fear. She did not think a girl should in any way fear the man whom she intended to marry.

In a word, she felt that Dan Stuart, despite his many attractions and sterling qualities, was a deal too cold-bloodedly, ruthlessly efficient—far too satisfied with and centered in: himself!

When she was in his presence, her love was paramount. But when they were apart, all her doubts, perplexities and worries came crowding back. Had Stuart been almost anyone save his own commanding, aloof and capable self, tonight at his office she would have confided in him instead of keeping her troubles to herself.

Finally, with a sigh and a little shrug, she rose from the rocker where she sat among the shadows of the veranda and entered the house to go to bed.

8

Dan Stuart looked the stranger over calmly, appraisingly, as he stood there with drawn gun beside the door. He saw that the man was huge, of elephantine stature; a giant whose brawny muscles possessed a mighty strength. He was clad in scuffed boots, faded Levi's, black woolen shirt open from neck to waistband, and a sweat-streaked calfskin vest, worn hair side out.

A battered black sombrero was pushed far back on his massive head. Beneath it his crag-like face was beefy and covered with a reddish stubble as though he had not shaved since yesterday. His grim-lipped mouth was clamped about the unlit stump of a black cigar.

"Hard," the sheriff's thoughts summed the stranger up. "Big as hell an' hard as flint."

"I guess likely you are doin' a heap of speculatin' as tuh who I am," the grim lips pushed the words out one by one around the cold cigar stump, slowly—almost wearily one might have thought. The long black eyes studied the sheriff inscrutably; no faintest flicker lighting the somber glance. "You are Dan Stuart, the sheriff?"

Stuart nodded.

Standing motionless just inside the door, the stranger appeared to meditate, yet there was no expression on his red-stubbled, crag-like countenance.

Slowly his glance roved round the bare little office, passing over Campero, lingering on the still form of Druce where it lay upon the bunk. The blank vacuity of his gaze did not alter; it was still inscrutable when he turned it back upon the Cibecue lawman.

"I'm Bruskell, the sheepman," his gruff voice explained. "Nephew to the ol' man over there."

Stuart's agate eyes looked hard and wary as he nodded. "I never tell a man I'm glad to meet him when he holds a gun on me while performin' the introduction," he said coldly.

Bruskell chuckled deep down in his great thick throat, and the intent black eyes with which he watched the sheriff did not waver, did not blink. "Fair enough," he gruffed, and his grim lips hardly moved. With an easy motion he returned his gun to the open, flapless holster thonged low on his left thigh. Stuart noted that when sheathed the weapon swung butt forward.

"Lot of murders in Cibecue lately—two too many," the big sheepman droned. "I rode in to see that Druce gets justice. He'll get it, too." His glance dropped briefly to the form of the dead herdsman. "What happened to Campero?"

Quietly, unhesitatingly, Stuart described the herdsman's killing. When he had finished, Bruskell's face was dark.

"Just so's to start you off with your best foot forward," the big stranger's voice rolled across the room like thunder, slow but heavy, "I'm goin' to tell you, Mister Stuart, who's behind these killin's. Campero an' my uncle were killed by them damned land-hawggin' cowmen. They've been on the prod, a-brewin' big medicine, ever since we got to Picture Rock with our sheep.

"This is a free country, Stuart, an' a sheepman is every inch as damned important as a cattleman—an' don't forget it. A sheepman's death hurts a sheepman's family just as much as a cattleman's hurts his kin. It's just as much a crime to kill a sheepman, accordin' to the law of this here state, as it is to kill a cowman. Now then, what do you aim to do about these killin's?"

"That," said Stuart evenly, "is my business. It's a concern of the sheriff's office, and said office is quite capable of takin' care of it—an' without any outside help. Is that clear, Bruskell?"

"Clear an' satisfactory." The big sheepman's voice came to a pause, then added slowly:

"There's one other little matter that I'd like to make plain, Sheriff. It's about our flocks. Them cowmen have started the usual cure for sheep troubles by killin'—"

"Not so fast," Stuart cut in. "You're bitin' off too big a mouthful when you say that. It's pure guesswork on your part, Bruskell, when you say these killings are the work of cowmen."

73

"Mebbe it is, mebbe not," Bruskell answered enigmatically. "But I know what I know an' I aim to act on it. Killin' sheepmen is quite a pleasant pastime for cattlemen, I've found. There ain't nothin' they like better unless it's runnin' off homesteaders.

"We've bought land in this country, Stuart, an'—we aim to use it. If we have to fight every cowman from here to Showlow, we're goin' to get our sheep onto our property—an' Gawd help the fools that try to stop us!"

"I've argued this business out with Druce when I stopped at your camp day before yesterday," Stuart's tone was calm, his drawling voice was soft. "Your uncle's death makes you the biggest owner in the pool. Now what you're aiming to do will, if you try to carry out your plans, result in another such bloody chapter to Arizona's history as the Tonto Basin fracas. It'll mean the deaths of a lot of innocent folks along with the guilty. I'll put the same proposition up to you that I made Caspar Druce."

"I wasn't at camp when you talked with Druce," Bruskell reminded him. "What was your proposition?"

"I'll pay you fellows once and a half again as much money as you paid—"

Bruskell waved the offer aside with a hamlike hand. "The pool is not interested in selling its Arizona property, Stuart. We're here an' by the

Almighty, here we stay! Come daylight, I'm shovin' our flocks across the Rim!"

A hoarse snarl tore the sudden silence that followed Bruskell's threat. A snarl that came from the intense blackness of the out-of-doors behind the sheepman's back. A snarl that dripped with venom, hate, and menace.

Bruskell, despite his great bulk, whirled swiftly, right hand dragging at his gun. Then his great frame went rigid as he found himself staring into the gaunt face and smouldering eyes of Jabe Broughton who stood, a big gun in either hand, just outside the open door.

"Go on, yuh pot-bellied sheepherder! Finish that draw so I can spill yore guts!" the cowman snarled across his leveled weapons. "Drive yore stinkin' sheep across the Rim, eh? Draw—damn yuh, draw!"

The air inside the Sheriff's Office appeared to be tightening up as though for some long-delayed explosion. But the explosion did not come.

"Humph!" Broughton snorted contemptuously after several dragging moments had passed in silence. Deliberately, suggestively, he pouched his heavy guns. "I mighta knowed it," he taunted. "Like all the rest of yore lousy breed, yuh're yaller as a mongrel pup!"

Not by the tiniest jerk of a muscle did Bruskell's face take on expression. The man seemed cold as ice. His long black eyes regarded Broughton with inscrutable intensity, never wavering a fraction at Jabe's insults. His silent, unblinking scrutiny enraged the cowman in much the same manner as a red rag does a bull.

Broughton's passionate high-boned face grew dark with fury, his lips writhed back from his yellowed teeth. He was at least a good four years older than Dorinda, and there was no resemblance between them such as one might expect to see between a brother and his sister. He was gaunt, rawboned and gangling, and just now his features were twisted in a vicious snarl. Only the sheriff's presence seemed to check his flaring passions.

"You—you—" his guns made threatening arcs, "yuh don't have tuh shove them hell-spawned sheep across the Rim, hombre! If yo're lookin' fer fight, jest start them woollies across this valley. I'll guarantee it'll be the las' thing yuh do on Gawd's green earth! Get me? Savvy? Us cowmen won't quit till we've stomped every yaller sheepman from the country!"

Bruskell's heavy face tightened around the cigar-stump. He nodded, his black eyes still inscrutable. "I expect I understand, Mister."

"Yuh better!" Broughton's rawboned figure was almost trembling, so great was his hate and fury. "Them two corpses over there is only a sample o' what'll happen if one of yore blattin' flocks sets foot inside the Cibecue! I'm a plain man an' I deal in plain talk, fella. Keep yore sheep where they are or we'll send every last one of yuh to hell on a shutter!"

Bruskell had listened to the cowman's tirade in silence. Now he spat on the dusty floor as though in defiance of Broughton's fiery warning.

A faint smile now tugged at his hard lips—the grin of an amused wolf. "I've listened to you, Mister. Now I'll say my say. You an' all the rest of the land-hawggin' cowmen in this man's valley can go plumb to hell, for all of me! Soon's it's light enough I'm takin' my sheep across the Rim!"

Slowly, distinctly in that silent room, the sheepman's defiant words shoved forth around the stump of black cigar. And as he stared straight into Broughton's smouldering eyes, his grim-lipped mouth retained its saturnine curve.

Eye to eye the two men stared.

Stuart watched them with a frown, saw the faint smile depart from the big sheepman's lips, leaving his red-stubbled face even more crag-like and inscrutable than it had been before.

Broughton's features drew tight with rage, his skin suffused with blood till it resembled the color of muddy wine.

Stuart stepped suddenly forward and his jaw was grim and hard.

"This wrangling has gone far enough," he drawled with dangerous softness, as he stepped between the belligerents. "Put them guns up, Jabe. . . . Put 'em up!"

Slowly, reluctantly, Broughton shortened his gaze to take in the sheriff. What he saw caused his smouldering eyes to narrow. One of Stuart's ivory-butted guns was in his hand. How it had got there, and when, Broughton did not know. But the significance of its gaping muzzle was perfectly plain, as was the hard, bleak light in the sheriff's agate eyes.

After a long glaring moment he pouched his heavy guns. Then his lips curled in a bitter sneer.

"Humph! Herdin' with the sheep again!" he sneered. "By cripes, Stuart, it's a wonder tuh me yuh don't shuck yore star an' go in fer raisin' the blattin' critters!"

Stuart's voice when he spoke was low, cold, even.

"Some day, Jabe, I reckon I'll have to kill you."

The sheriff's words contained no breath of threat, no bluster. They constituted a soft-spoken, even statement of a simple thought. The air seemed suddenly chilled in the little room, though outside it was getting steadily warmer as dawn drew near.

Broughton's face looked a trifle less ruddy than it had a moment before. He moved his hands away from his hips, made pretense that his neckerchief needed adjusting.

"Listen careful, gents, an' remember what I tell

you," Stuart's glance, suddenly vacuous, held both men in its radius. "I want you boys to stop champin' at the bit; quit suckin' wind. There ain't goin' to be no war in Cibecue Valley. And the knife artist that tallied three notches last night is goin' to get all the law allows."

No changing expression betrayed the sheepman's thoughts. No spoken word revealed his intentions. For all the signs of hearing Bruskell gave, the sheriff might not have spoken.

But not so, Broughton.

Though the cowman was careful to keep his hands away from the region of his hips, his hot-tempered personality would not let him rest without a vocal jibe.

"Yore talk sounds mighty big, Dan Stuart, but it ain't scarin' me any," his black brows twisted down in an ugly scowl. "You've changed a uncommon lot since we voted yuh into the sheriff's office, an' yuh sold yore ranch. But yuh ain't foolin' me any. You're sidin' with the sheepmen!

"An' lemme tell yuh somethin' else, fella. Sheepmen ain't wanted around the Circle B. From now on you steer clear, hear me? My sister don't want no truck with no dang wool-grower!"

9

Bruskell chuckled deep down in his great thick throat.

"Oh, you're positive of that, I expect?"

Jabe Broughton stared. Was the fellow crazy?

"Better not let me catch yuh hangin' around," he threatened. "My sister is a cowman's daughter— she don't want no kind of truck with sheepmen nor the friends of sheepmen!"

"Then how," Bruskell chuckled in saturnine mirth, "do you account for your precious sister's handkerchief being found beside the body of Caspar Druce in the camp at Picture Rock?"

For just an instant there was a flicker of startled surprise in Stuart's agate glance. Then the old veil of caution fell once more across his eyes and left them hard and wary. Left them studying Jabe Broughton.

A bombshell could have caused no greater consternation than was pictured at that moment on the cowman's high-boned face. His mouth hung open with surprise, his eyes betrayed amazement, incredulity, wrath. Then his lips curled back from his yellow teeth in an ugly scowl, and there was a murderous glare in his bloodshot eyes.

"Dang you, Bruskell, for a lyin' polecat!" Jabe's hoarse voice was afire with the fury of his passion.

His gaunt, rawboned figure sagged swiftly to a crouch. Palms downward, his hands were spread, their fingers talon-like, above the polished butts of his holstered heavy guns. "Either show me the handkerchief, or get out that gun!"

Something in Bruskell's enigmatic glance, in the angles of his beefy, crag-like face or in the tilt of his heavy jaw, gave hint of a saturnine inner mirth. Yet his eyes betrayed no feeling; his sleepy lids lay across their black depths in a lazy unblinking stare.

"C'mon, yuh yeller pup," growled Broughton in a vicious snarl; "Produce that handkerchief or unloose that gun! I don't give a shuck which, but do one or t'other quick!"

Once again the air in the scantily-furnished office was tightening up, becoming brittle, rarified, cold. Once again destruction and tragedy seemed to be hovering close, but awaiting their cue to stalk across the scene.

The sheepman seemed unaffected by Broughton's taunting words; he continued to regard the cowman with his steady unblinking gaze. "I expect," he said slowly, pushing his words out around the stump of his black cigar, "that you'll have to get the sheriff to produce it if you're real set on seein' it. I ain't never had my hands on it, personal—but I guess Mister Stuart will be able to tell you where it is."

Watching the two men with guarded gaze, Stuart said in an even voice:

"I reckon you're mistaken, Bruskell. *I* haven't got any of Miss Broughton's handkerchiefs."

Bruskell grinned faintly. "I guess there's one around here someplace, Stuart."

Jabe Broughton stared from one to the other and, though still angry, there was bewilderment on his high-boned features.

"What is this, a game? C'mon, now; either I see that handkerchief or I'm gonna get me a sheepman's hide tuh nail on my barn door."

Stuart was doing some fast thinking. How in the devil did Bruskell know about Dorinda's handkerchief that he had removed from Campero's pocket? Plainly, there was more to this than met the eye. There was something mighty screwy about this handkerchief business. Had Bruskell somehow managed to see him burning the bit of cambric? Or was he guessing? And if he was guessing, what information was he in possession of to give a basis to his guess-work?

Yet no twitching muscle or change of color in his face conveyed to the others the chaotic turmoil of his thoughts. His face was calm and confident, and his grip on the ivory-handled gun was steady as he said:

"I think this wrangling has gone just about far enough, gentlemen. If it will seem more satisfactory or conclusive, or if it will relieve your feelings any, you are both at liberty to search this office at any time you find convenient. But we'll have no more of this wild *habla*. I—"

Broughton broke in with a savage snarl:

"I've heard enough of this chin-music. Bruskell, you're a dirty, polecat liar!"

In the border country and the wild fastnesses of Arizona, the term "liar" has long been a fighting epithet. For one man to hurl such a term into the teeth of another is to invite gunplay and quick extinction to the man whose trigger finger is a shade too slow in squeezing steel.

For a long second, Bruskell stared across the silence. Then his hand went jerking hipward, Broughton's following suit.

What might have happened in the next instant, had the sheriff not leaped forward, will probably never be known. Yet there can be no doubt but that guns would have flamed and, flaming at that close range, new graves leveled atop Boot Hill.

But the sheriff leaped, smoothly, swiftly, accurately, and his gun-barrel came flashing down in a glinting arc across Jabe Broughton's head. For a breathless instant the cowman stood there, swaying on his feet. Then his knees let go and he crumpled, fell forward on his face.

Gun held ready, Stuart flashed a swift glance at Bruskell.

The big sheepman seemed not to have moved a fraction, yet his heavy gun was in his hand. With a soft chuckle he slid it back inside its sheath. "Nice work, Stuart."

But the sheriff did not return his grin. The hot blood was pounding stormily through his arteries. There was a challenge in his voice:

"How did you know Dorinda Broughton's handkerchief was found beside the body of Caspar Druce," his agate eyes stared hard at the sheepman's face, "and knowing it, why did you make that crazy crack in front of Jabe?"

"Answerin' yore last question first, I said that to egg Broughton on to drawing first."

"And you thought that with Jabe's gun coming out of leather you still could beat him to the squeeze?" there was incredulity in Stuart's tones.

"I figgered it was worth a gamble," Bruskell said.

"Well, all I got to say," remarked Stuart drily, "is that it's uncommon lucky for you I jumped in an' batted him down when I saw him reaching for his guns. Jabe Broughton, in case you don't know it, is one of the fastest gents in this valley at unlimbering a forty-five!"

"Well, in that case I'll say I'm a heap obliged to you for savin' my life," the sheepman's drawl was mocking. "It ain't every day a man gets the chance to see a young cow-prodder riskin' his life to save a sheepman."

"Don't make no mistake, Bruskell. I'd have done the same for any man under the circumstances. I don't want to see trouble get started in this county.

If you fellows had got your guns to spouting, it wouldn't have made any difference to the county which of you got killed. Regardless of how it had turned out, it would have been a match in the powderkeg to this sheep an' cattle feud that's workin' up. I've got enough trouble on my hands figuring out who killed your uncle, Campero an'—"

Stuart broke off abruptly. Better keep Cal Broughton's name out of the death roll, for a while. He reverted to his former question:

"How did you know about Dorinda's handkerchief being found beside Druce's body?"

Bruskell met the sheriff's gaze, but did not answer immediately. He seemed to be deliberating. He acted neither surprised nor intimidated by the lawman's accusing manner. Indeed he seemed entirely unperturbed. Rolling his cigar stump to the opposite corner of his mouth, he said:

"Because I saw it there."

"You—you saw it there?"

Bruskell nodded, and once again the faint grin curved his grim-lipped mouth.

"Yep—blue cambric, it was. Had her initials in one corner. Campero picked it up and shoved it in a pocket before he picked up Señor Druce and lashed him on his old blue roan."

"Yeah?" Stuart's tone was curt, livened with suspicion. "Where was you when you saw all this?"

Bruskell chuckled lazily, deep down in his great thick throat. "I heard Campero comin' about three minutes 'fore he hove in sight. I must of arrived a good five minutes ahead of him. When I heard him comin' I got out of sight. *I* didn't know who was comin' an' I didn't aim to have some jasper shovin' a knife between *my* ribs."

"That part is natural enough," Stuart admitted, with reservations. "Where did you hide while Campero was around?"

"Inside the tent."

"Druce's tent?"

Bruskell nodded.

"Campero," said Stuart slowly, "told me that when he got to camp there was a light on in Druce's tent."

"There was."

"An' you mean to tell me you stayed inside the tent while Campero was pokin' around outside, and he never knew you was there?" disbelief marked Stuart's tone.

"I didn't say he didn't know I was there," Bruskell's grin was lazy, easy, unforced. "He knew someone was inside all right because he saw my shadow. It showed on the front wall of the tent when I got to a place where I could see what was goin' on outside. But Campero was always a cautious sort of hombre. He was careful not to look inside."

Stuart eyed the big sheepman coldly, disbelievingly. His tone, when next he spoke, was vibrant with cold suspicion: "When you saw who it was, that it was one of your own herders outside, why didn't you go out and talk with him?"

Bruskell eyed Stuart unblinkingly. "How did I know but what Campero had stabbed my uncle, gone away, then remembered something he had forgotten and come back for it? He *might* have been the killer."

"But you didn't think he was or you wouldn't have stayed inside the tent," Stuart countered swiftly. "You've got guts, Bruskell. That story don't wash with me. Here's another thing—You claim you got to the camp some five minutes before Campero put in an appearance. Five minutes would give you ample time to stab your uncle an' then hide inside the tent."

"I reckon," Bruskell's eyes stared calmly into Stuart's, straight, unflinching, "five minutes would be plenty of time. But if I'd stabbed my uncle, I hope you don't think I'd be fool enough to linger in the vicinity with nothin' between me an' discovery but a sheet of canvas."

"On the contrary," Stuart said, "I think you might be clever enough. It's all a question of judgment an' viewpoint. Knowing that the majority of people in this valley would reason as you just did, on the surface of it, staying inside that tent after murdering your uncle would look like the craziest thing you could do. For that very reason I should regard it as a brilliant stroke on your part. An' I honestly believe you've got nerve enough an' sense enough to see it that way."

"Well," Bruskell grinned lazily, "I'm obliged for the compliment, sheriff. But I expect you are overratin' my nerve a little an' my judgment a whole lot. Besides, I never carry a knife, so I think you'll find it pretty hard to prove I murdered uncle Caspar," as the gruff voice trailed off, Bruskell's lips widened in a sardonic quirk.

"You're a pretty shrewd customer, Mister Sheepman," Stuart's voice held a note of grudging admiration. "Who are you, anyway? You're not an ordinary sheepherder—you've had education. You've got brains and you know how to use 'em. I can't figure out why a man of your ability and discernment should have seen fit to throw in with a man of Druce's caliber."

"Perhaps you are forgetting that Caspar Druce was my uncle, Stuart."

"No—I'm forgetting nothing. How long would you say Druce had been dead when you came across his body?"

"I don't know much about such things," Bruskell answered thoughtfully. "I'd say not more than half an hour."

"What happened to the knife he was stabbed with? It wasn't in the body when Campero brought it in."

10

"It was not in the body when I found it, either."

Stuart looked straight into Bruskell's long black eyes.

"I should hate to find it necessary to call you a liar, Mister," his soft drawl emerged through tautened lips.

Bruskell looked straight into Stuart's level eyes. "I should hate for you to have occasion to, Sheriff. Howsomever, I'm handin' you the truth. There was no knife in my uncle's body when I found it before his tent."

"We'll let it go like that, for the moment," Stuart said, his muscles relaxing. "Why had you returned to the camp at Picture Rock when you were stationed at the camp below Brush Mountain?"

Once again Bruskell appeared to meditate, holding silent communion with himself. "I don't expect I'll answer that question," his gruff voice came at last. "A lawyer would say it might tend to incriminate me."

Stuart, studying the man thoughtfully, realized full well that here was no ordinary sheepman. He had brains. He had cold courage, too—a thing not frequently encountered among men of his occupation, or so Dan Stuart thought. Bruskell was possessed of a forceful, potent personality.

Intelligent, courageous, calm and efficient, master of himself at all times, this nephew of Caspar Druce presented an enigma.

Stuart decided to reserve judgment—decided to give the man plenty of rope.

A groan came from Broughton's prostrate form.

"Guess you'd better be goin', Bruskell. Looks as though Jabe was about to return to this vale of wailin' tears. You will oblige me by bein' gone when he comes to. And, another thing, I'd take it kindly if you'd see that the sheepmen hold their flocks right where they are for the time being."

"Now, look here, Stuart." Bruskell's black eyes gleamed strangely. "You know very well that we've got to get our sheep onto our property near Showlow at the earliest possible minute. You know that we'll never get them there without crossin' the Cibecue an' the Tonto Rim. That request of yours, all things considered, ain't hardly fair."

"I know it. But you know how I got roped in on this, I reckon. Your uncle pulled a slick one on me. So you'd ought to be able to see my angle, too. Keep your sheep where they are till I give the word or there'll be bad trouble."

For a long moment Bruskell stared at the sheriff's lean jutting jaw; at the firm, tight-pinched mouth above it, and at the lawman's agate eyes. He nodded slowly. "All right, Stuart. I'll trail along with you for a spell."

No change of expression flitted across Dan Stuart's face, to show whether or not he was pleased with Bruskell's attitude. No expression told whether or not the sheepman had managed to quiet the sheriff's suspicions of Bruskell's connection with the mysterious death of Caspar Druce. "There'll be inquests here this afternoon or tomorrow. It won't be necessary nor advisable for you to be in town."

"I see your point," Bruskell answered smoothly. "Guess you've heard about Broughton sending out of the valley for gun fighters? . . . No? Well, he's sent for one that I know of. Keep your eyes peeled. The sheepmen with me don't dare trust you, an' you can't blame 'em for that, Stuart. I don't reckon the cowmen are trustin' you overmuch these days, either. Better keep your irons loose an' your eyes open."

"I'm friendly to all square-shooters," Stuart said quietly. "It don't make no difference to me whether they're cowmen or sheepmen. All I'm tryin' to do is prevent trouble in the Cibecue. I'm tryin' to do my duty as I see it."

Bruskell nodded and left the office.

After the sheepman's departure Stuart poured a cup of water from the earthenware jug beside his desk and splashed its contents over Broughton's face.

The cowman groaned, spluttered, gasped and sat up painfully. As he met the sheriff's cold glance he swore. He was still swearing when he got to his feet.

"Get it all out of your system," Stuart advised. "When you get through I'll talk."

Broughton, glaring, abruptly grinned. "Shucks, Stuart, I guess I don't hold it against yuh. Likely in yore place I'd of done the same thing. I sort of lost my head or I wouldn't have reached for my guns. I jest can't stand a sheepman's guts, that's all. Jest the sight of one riles me uncommon bad. An' when he tried to make out Dorinda's handkerchief was found— Aw, shucks! Let's forget it."

Stuart was willing, and said so.

"Cripes! My head feels like a mule with sixteen feet done kicked it," Cal Broughton's son said with a grimace. "Got anythin' I can put on it?"

Stuart produced a bottle of liniment and applied it generously to the cowman's lacerated scalp. Broughton swore considerable during the process, but seemed to feel a little better when the sheriff put the bottle away.

Stuart realized that he really ought to tell Jabe about his father's death, but feeling that this was an inopportune time, said nothing about it. Young Broughton would find out soon enough, anyway, he thought. The cowmen would go hog-wild when they heard of it, he feared. Aloud he said:

"Bruskell has agreed to hold his sheep at Picture

Rock a spell longer. I expect the cowmen to leave them be."

Broughton scowled, then smiled. "Yeah, we won't bother 'em as long as they don't try to cross the Cibecue. All we want is to keep 'em from spoilin' our grass."

As the Circle B man turned to go, Stuart said: "There'll be an inquest on these dead sheepmen— probably sometime this afternoon. You may be wanted. I wish you'd stay in town until I get a chance to talk with the Coroner."

Broughton nodded and departed without further speech.

Stuart went over and sank down behind his desk. The sheriff of Navajo County was weary and baffled. His main problem was to keep trouble from Cibecue Valley, but how could he hope to do it with an unknown assassin on the prod? For the 'steenth time he wondered who could be the unknown killer of Cibecue. . . .

When Jabe Broughton left the Sheriff's Office and turned his steps toward the Warwhoop Hotel to bed down for the next few hours in an effort to make up some of his lost sleep, the eastern sky was already brightening with the first fiery banners of the rising sun.

Deep in Jabe's soul there were fiery banners equally bright. The way the sheriff had put it over on him before the cowmen last night in the

Bucket of Blood was humiliating, to say the least. But this was as nothing to the humiliation of Stuart's act in knocking him down and out before a hated sheepman. Deep in Jabe's vengeful soul burned a longing to get even; to humble Stuart or to kill him for the insults he had put upon him.

Ever since Stuart had come to the Valley two years ago, looking for a range, Jabe had hated and envied him in secret. When Stuart had bought the S Bar 4 near Showlow, above the Rim, Jabe had thought to see the last of him. Vain hope. Stuart had run against him in the Navajo County race for the sheriff's office, beating him two to one. And as if all this was not enough, Jabe felt sure that Dorinda was falling in love with the uppity devil.

As he strode toward the hotel, a long frame structure next door to the Bucket of Blood, Broughton cursed savagely. How he hated Stuart! How he envied the man's impenetrable calm, his confident assurance, his efficiency! But he would humble him yet. He would somehow find a way to make the sheriff crawl!

His thoughts turned to the dusty stranger he had seen in the saloon last night. Who was the fellow? Where had he come from? Where was he going?

Ah! There was an idea for you! Broughton's eyes gleamed with sudden thought. Yes, that stranger! It was an idea worth careful consideration; an idea which might be made to yield big dividends. Should hard luck come upon the sheriff, the dusty stranger might be made to play the role of goat. . . .

In a vastly lighter frame of mind, his weariness and his aching head alike forgotten, Jabe Broughton climbed the hotel steps and entered the dingy lobby. No clerk was behind the desk at this early hour, so he reached across, grabbed a key from the rack and went clumping up the narrow stairs.

11

After sitting at his desk for some time, Dan Stuart found his thoughts turning to the complications resulting from his sale of the S Bar 4. He had bought the ranch at a reasonable price two years ago. But for some time beef prices had been low and he had been unable to see any immediate prospect of said prices going higher.

Then had come the Navajo County elections. The people had voted him the sheriff's job, which he had won with a two-to-one margin over Jabe Broughton. He had decided to sell his cattle ranch and, in furthering this decision, had advertised in several Arizona and New Mexican papers.

A short time after his ad had appeared, he had received a letter from a man named Hoskins— Lemuel B. Hoskins. This gentleman claimed to be secretary to a New Mexican livestock organization known as the Tucumcari Pool. Mr. Hoskins said his people were interested in the S Bar 4 and intimated that he would like to look the property over. Stuart had invited him to come and inspect the ranch at his convenience.

A week later Hoskins had appeared at the S Bar 4, near Showlow. Lemuel B. was an odd sort of chap who reminded the sheriff of a pale worm that had stayed overlong below a drain pipe.

A lanky man who dressed in black store duds and talked incessantly of Arizona—"the wonderland of America." He reveled in its prehistoric ruins, he fairly went into hysterics over its Indian pueblos. He could talk for hours on the Petrified Forest and Grand Canyon.

Waxing exceedingly voluble, he told Stuart of the citrus fruits, dates, grain, lettuce, cantaloupe, cotton and alfalfa for which certain sections of the state were held in world-wide esteem.

He spoke of Arizona's copper mines, describing them in glowing terms as being among the richest in the universe; he spoke of the gold and silver mines and the quarries of onyx and marble.

During one of their many talks, held while riding over the property which the newly-elected sheriff hoped to dispose of at a profit, Mr. Hoskins told Stuart that he had been astounded to learn that practically every member of the cactus family—including even the giant saguaros that grew to a height of forty and fifty feet—abounded in Arizona.

He spoke of the reclamation project going on under government supervision in the Salt River Valley, describing it in glowing terms as one of the marvels of the day.

He knew all about the coming of the first Spaniard to Arizona back in 1539, one Friar Marcos de Niza, and took pride in recounting the worthy friar's hair-raising experiences—which the sheriff had no doubt were largely a figment of his fertile mind.

He described the great Pueblo revolt of 1860 as vividly as though he had been a witness to the scenes he recounted.

Indeed Mr. Lemuel B. Hoskins was a source of vast and astounding knowledge on the subject of Arizona—"the wonderland of America." He not only could, but did talk for hours upon its salient features. But when it came to talk of ranching and cattle raising, Lemuel B. was singularly reticent.

But, bemused by the great line of gab slung out by the black-garbed stranger who described himself as secretary to the Tucumcari Pool, Dan Stuart had found no time in which to become suspicious of the Hoskins reticence with regard to affairs of ranch and range.

After a week spent in going over the S Bar 4, Hoskins had declared himself satisfied and had asked Stuart to name his price. Stuart named it and Hoskins paid down a cashier's check on the Cowmen's Bank of Tucumcari for five thousand dollars to bind the deal, promising to pay the balance within ten days. When the tenth day came rolling round Mr. Hoskins produced a second cashier's check covering the balance due, and the following day Dan Stuart moved out, several thousands of dollars to the good.

Several days later it came to Stuart's ears that

Hoskins was selling off the bulk of the S Bar 4 cattle, and dismissing the majority of the punchers. They were being replaced with new hands, one of the discharged cowboys explained to Stuart. These tales caused the sheriff a vague uneasiness.

When he heard that Hoskins was remodeling the buildings, and erecting several entirely new structures, the sheriff's uneasiness was no longer vague. Definite alarm had him in its grip, though outwardly he remained his usual calm and confident self. There was, however, one noticeable difference apparent in Stuart—he became more and more close-mouthed, less and less inclined to talk and laughter.

Then came the day when Druce appeared at Picture Rock with his bleating flocks, his herdsmen, camp helpers and so forth. Immediately on hearing of the arrival of sheepmen at Blue House Mountain, Stuart had left Holbrook poste haste for Cibecue Valley. Directly upon his arrival he had gone to the camp at Picture Rock, seeking Druce and an explanation of his presence in what for years had been undisputed cow country.

With a jeering laugh, Druce had explained that he was president of the Tucumcari Pool, and that he and his fellow members of the organization were en route to the S Bar 4—their Arizona property.

The sheepman's revelation had been a bitter

blow to Stuart's pride and integrity. His open trust of his fellow men had suffered a most disastrous shock when he realized how he had been hoodwinked into selling his ranch to a syndicate of sheepmen.

In an attempt to rectify his mistake, the sheriff had offered to re-purchase the S Bar 4 at once-and-a-half the price he had received from the Pool. But Druce had laughed at him. The Tucumcari Pool, Stuart was informed, was an organization of buyers. The selling of property held no allure for them.

Stuart, holding his anger in check, had pointed out the probable feelings of the Cibecue cowmen when they should learn that a sheepman had bought property above the Rim. The cowmen, he said, would never permit sheep to cross the valley. If Druce attempted to take his flocks across there would be war—bloody, disastrous war for all concerned.

Druce had scoffed loudly. He had been through range wars before; knew all about them and felt no fear of the threatened war in Cibecue Valley. If things got too hot, he pointed out with a triumphant grin, the government would step in as they'd done in Tonto Basin. The sheepmen had a right to cross this valley—it was mainly government land to which the cowmen held but squatters rights.

Stuart had come back to town filled with chagrin

and resentment. He was determined to prevent this threatened war, for which he felt himself alone responsible, no matter what the cost.

Then, to aggravate the already serious situation, had come these ghastly murders!

Stuart slowly rose from the chair behind his desk. For a time he stood there motionless, only his keen roving eyes stabbing about the scantily-furnished office showing the tension under which he labored.

A great green fly moving languidly across the surface of his desk caught his attention. It would walk a few steps in more or less aimless fashion, then pause to scratch the back of its large-eyed head with one of its several feet. Stuart watched it in silent fascination till, with a sudden loud buzz, it droned away.

Slowly, then, chin on chest, he began to pace the floor.

Who, he wondered, would be the most likely to benefit by the death of Druce? He was convinced in his own mind that Druce had been the first victim of the unknown knifer of Cibecue. What did the fact signify, if anything?

Answering the first question, it might seem at first glance that the cattlemen had the most interest in removing Druce. And the biggest cattleman in this country had been Cal Broughton. But Cal Broughton, too, was dead.

Had Broughton killed Druce, and one of the sheepmen killed Broughton in revenge?

No, this theory seemed a bit far-fetched. In the first place Cal Broughton, had he wanted to kill Druce, would never have resorted to a knife. Of this, Dan Stuart felt sure.

Eliminating Cal Broughton from the possible killers of Druce, who was left?

The sheriff thought the possibles over carefully. There was Vic Tyrone with his red-rimmed eyes and scarred forehead and drink-engendered rages. There was the dead man's nephew, Bruskell, the enigmatic sheepman, with his sleepy-lidded glance, his black cigar stump, his speedy ham-like hands and grim-lipped mouth. There was Jabe Broughton, the hot-tempered son of the murdered Cal, like his father, a hater of sheep and sheepmen. And finally there was the mysterious dusty stranger. Possibly there were others, but these were the men who flashed across the sheriff's mental vision.

Vic Tyrone was ambitious. Stuart thought the man had an itch for power and fame; an overweening desire to extend his holdings. Such a desire might be served by a range war, for such a fracas—as the sheriff well knew—could be made highly profitable to a man of easy conscience and a ready running iron. Too, Tyrone, on general principle disliked all sheepmen and was not a bit bashful in openly saying so.

Bruskell, Stuart knew less than nothing about. He was a stranger here like his uncle and the rest of the Tucumcari Pool. But Stuart was of the opinion that Bruskell was hard and callous; an intelligent man who knew how to mask his emotions and control his temper. A dangerous man, and deep. There might be many reasons why Bruskell should desire his uncle's death.

Jabe Broughton might kill Druce out of revenge for the death of his father. But Jabe did not yet know of Big Cal Broughton's death, and besides, it was Stuart's conviction that Cal Broughton's killing had followed that of Druce and preceded that of Campero, the Mexican herder. It seemed to the sheriff that Bruskell was far more likely to have done the killing than young Jabe, hotheaded though the latter was.

As for the dusty stranger—Well, Stuart realized that he knew nothing of the man, nor of his reasons for being at this particular time in Cibecue. For all he knew to the contrary, the dusty stranger from afar might have ridden to the Cibecue for the sole purpose of slaying Druce and Broughton.

This theory, however, brought the sheriff up against the "grim secret" angle. He could not conceive of any secret of any moment being shared by Caspar Druce and Big Cal Broughton. No secret, at any rate, which would necessitate their sudden deaths.

His thoughts abruptly, wonderingly, took another tack.

Might there not be a third faction at work in the Cibecue; one siding with neither sheep nor cattle, but secretly working against them both? A faction so anxious to precipitate a sheep and cattle war as to resort to downright murder?

Yes, such a faction, the sheriff admitted to himself, might well exist. In any cowland paradise there was always the chance that some far-sighted rascal, utterly unscrupulous and ruthless in the furthering of his ends, might seek to set his neighbors at each other's throats in the hope that ultimately he might rule the land alone.

Certainly it was a possibility that ought to be considered.

Still restlessly pacing the floor, the sheriff's thoughts turned to Bruskell. If the big sheepman had been the first innocent person to reach Druce after the man was stabbed, why had he not admitted it at once? Why had he apparently sought to conceal the fact? Why had he not emerged and spoken to Campero? Why should he wish to let Campero think he had been first to discover the crime?

What more was the inscrutable Bruskell holding back?

Was Bruskell, after all, the unknown killer of Cibecue? He seemed big enough, and hard enough, and confident enough to be the wielder of an assassin's blade. He was calm, self-possessed, courageous, deep. A man whose deep strength enabled him to conceal all emotion whenever he so-willed. If he had killed his uncle, what had been his reason for killing Cal Broughton? Or had some other hand driven the blade that had killed Big Cal?

"A hellish mess if ever I saw one!" Stuart growled, as he dropped heavily, wearily, to the chair behind his desk. But hardly had he seated himself than curiosity to examine the knife that had killed Campero drove him across the room.

Beside Campero's body Stuart stopped with widening eyes. The knife was gone!

Amazement chased the stony look from his glance, incredulity was stamped upon his features as he bent above the dead man.

There was the wound in Campero's chest—but the knife whose blade had inflicted it was no longer in the body.

Stuart's hands flung out in a gesture of bewilderment. His eyes, quick with questions, searched the room. There was no sign of the fatal weapon anywhere. It seemed to have vanished as though it had never been.

Stuart swore with feeling, bitterly. He blamed himself for not having placed the knife some-where in safe-keeping. He reproached himself with criminal neglect. But it did not bring back the vanished bit of steel and bone.

Someone had made a fool of him; and the someone was either Tyrone, Bruskell, or Broughton, for no one else had been in the office since Campero's death.

Who would wish to remove the bit of evidence represented by the fatal blade? Who indeed except the murderer himself? Or, possibly, someone trying to protect him. But the man who took it upon himself to make off with the missing knife was, in Stuart's estimation, undoubtedly the mysterious killer. And just as certainly, to Stuart's way of thinking, that man was either Tyrone, who had been here first; Bruskell, who had entered second; or Jabe Broughton, who had been the last to enter and the last to leave!

The sheriff's agate eyes grew slitted, his lean, square jaw clenched grimly. It did not seem to him that any one of the men had had ample opportunity to steal that knife. Yet it was gone—plainly someone must have taken it!

"Knifing," he muttered hoarsely, "is a sheepman's way."

Again he started pacing, then halted, struck by a sudden thought.

It was possible that this series of sudden killings arose from something in the past—something to which the sheriff had no key. Vengeance, maybe.

But that detracted nothing from the probability that one of the three recent visitors was the guilty man. There was no conceivable reason for anyone to remove the fatal weapon unless the remover was himself the killer, or—less likely— knew and was endeavoring to shield the killer.

The sheriff tensed at the sound of clumping boots on the board walk outside the office door. Someone was coming. With his hands curled round the ivory butts of his holstered six-guns, Dan Stuart turned.

A moment later the door was flung open. Nip Wingate, followed by another man, came in, leaving the door open. The man with the deputy was Bert Allen, the Coroner. He was a somber looking fellow with a sallow, unbronzed face.

Stuart nodded curtly. "Sorry to get you out of bed so early, Allen. Did you remove Broughton's body from the alley?"

Allen growled an affirmative, turned his attention to the two still forms.

After several moments, Stuart, unable longer to contain himself, asked:

"Well, which of the three was stabbed first, Allen?"

Allen looked up from his examination of the sheepmen's bodies long enough to growl: "Druce," and immediately went on with his examination, paying no further attention to the sheriff for several moments.

Nip Wingate was filling his blackened pipe, preparatory to smoking. He glanced at Stuart, caught his eye:

"It's dang lucky, by cripes, that I thought tuh remove the knife that killed Campero—" he began, then stopped when he saw the strange expression on Stuart's staring face.

12

Dan Stuart glared at his deputy with cold, hard agate eyes. His lean-waisted figure, in blue flannel shirt and faded Levi's, taut and erect. His fists clenched at his sides. Cords of muscle stood out along his lean brown jaw, a whisper of escaping breath came from his parted lips.

"Well!" exasperation stamped the word. "So you are the gent that walked off with that blade!"

"Humph," Wingate said as he finished pressing the tobacco into the bowl of his pipe, "you sound a bit peeved, Dan. You wasn't huntin' for that ear-gotcher, was yuh?"

"No," sardonically, "not at all! Do you know, Mister Wingate, that I been suspectin' a number of gents of makin' off with that knife right under my nose, an' had just about concluded that the hombre that hooked it must be the killer? Well, I can tell you that them has been my thoughts."

"Who yuh been suspectin'?" Allen asked, curiously.

"There's been three gents in here since Campero died, aside from Wingate; said gents being Tyrone, Bruskell an' Jabe Broughton," Stuart said, and dropped wearily into his chair.

"Bruskell came in here quiet as a mouse right after you pulled out, Nip. First thing I knew of him bein' here was when I turned around an' saw him standing in the door with a gun bent on me. He dropped in to tell me that the cowmen are back of these killings. Apparently he ain't aware that Cal Broughton is one of the victims. I can't see why any cowman would find it profitable to stab Big Cal, unless he's simply tryin' to stir up trouble."

"Hell," said Wingate, his wrinkled lips writhed in a sneer, "knifing is a lousy sheepman's trick! No cowman would use a knife on a fella!"

"That's what I've been thinking," Stuart admitted. "But we can't be sure of that."

"Can you name a cowman in this valley that would be guilty of killing with a knife?" asked Allen sharply.

Stuart looked at the sallow-faced Coroner. "No," he said, quietly, "I don't know as I can. But that doesn't mean that no cattleman in the Cibecue would do so. Nothin' like this has ever happened around here before, so far as I know. It's what Bruskell would call 'unprecedented'."

Scowls crossed his companions' faces at mention of the sheepman. To them, it seemed that Stuart was entirely too friendly with the sheep interests for a man who had once run cattle. It might be, they thought, that after all there was something in the cowmen's altered feelings toward the sheriff—some warrant for their regarding him with hostility.

Stuart sensed what was going on in his companions' minds, but said nothing. His expression remained the same as he regarded them with unwavering glance.

"Did you learn anything, Nip, when you went over the alley where Broughton was stabbed?" he asked.

"No!" growled Wingate, and puffed moodily on his wheezing pipe.

"Clues," remarked Allen, "was scarcer than hen's teeth aboard ship! By the way, Stuart, I hear Jabe Broughton has sent outside for a top-notch gun slinger."

"So I've heard." Stuart looked them over thoughtfully. "So you didn't uncover anything out there in that alley, eh?"

Allen frowned. Wingate cleared his throat:

"We spent most of our time huntin' the knife that killed Cal Broughton," he muttered grimly. "But we didn't have no luck. It's plumb vanished! I reckon the killer came back after it, not feelin' anxious to leave any trademark."

A gloomy silence stole over the sheriff's office then. Wingate puffed his pipe. Allen squinted out the open office door, watching the sunrise. Stuart rested his elbows on the desk, square-jawed chin cupped in his upthrust hands, staring fixedly into space.

"Whoever this killer is," Stuart said, at last, "he's a nervy cuss. He proved it when he slung the knife through the office window and killed Campero. He proved it again when he lingered in that alley to take a shot at me. And still again when he went back after the knife with which he killed Cal Broughton."

Wingate nodded moodily.

"But that's no help," Allen grumbled. "If anything, it only makes it harder for us to nail him. But I don't think that it's bravery that caused him to do those things. To my notion fear is the drivin' impulse. He did those things because he was afraid not to do them. He shot at you, hoping to rub you out. Had he succeeded, the chances are that a less implacable bloodhound would have been put on his trail."

"Thanks for the compliment," Stuart grinned mirthlessly.

"The killer went back after the knife that killed Broughton, because he was afraid it might identify him," Allen went on, warming up to his subject. "He threw the knife through the window killing Campero because he was afraid of what Campero might be about to reveal—proving that Campero could have told us something interesting."

Pausing, the Coroner stared at Stuart, then added: "Furthermore, it has been my experience that knives are nearly always the weapons of cowards."

Wingate nodded his agreement with Allen's

theory. "My notion, too," he said, blowing out a great cloud of smoke.

But Stuart stuck to his point. "I can't agree," he said quietly. "I believe the killer is a man of resource, a man of iron courage and grim determination. A man who had a set purpose and a powerful motive in killing Druce. It is my theory that he killed Campero, as you say, to silence him. And it seems to me that the same reason may hold good in the case of Big Cal Broughton. Though of the last, I'm not real certain."

His face was grim as he stared levelly at his companions. "After Wingate left in search of you, Allen, I stepped to the door a moment and stood looking out into the darkness. Someone took a hasty shot at me—with a rifle, I imagine. He was over across the road behind the corrals, I think. I'm going to look around over there pretty soon. I don't expect I'll find much, but I'm aimin' to take a look."

Wingate and the Coroner eyed Stuart in questioning silence.

"Does that look like the work of a man driven by fear?"

"Sure it does," Allen grunted. "He was scared you might get onto him. So he got his rifle and laid out there in the shadows by the corral waitin' for you to step out the door where he could get a shot at you without tippin' his hand."

"He's a pretty good shot," the sheriff said. "He

113

come within two inches of gettin' me. Well, you may be right. But I still cotton to the notion the fellow has guts."

"If he has, I wouldn't count Jabe Broughton among the fellows who might be the killer," Allen retorted.

"Why? Jabe Broughton's got plenty of nerve."

"Plenty of wind, too," Wingate added. "Jabe's all talk an' bluster. He totes two guns an' only shoots with his right hand—couldn't hit a barn door with his left. So what's he want to wear two guns for, unless he's tryin' to put on a front?"

"The trouble with Jabe," grinned Allen, "is that he's sufferin' from a inferiority complex."

"Well, I'm not especially considering any of them three right now," said Stuart. "It was when I thought one of them had taken the knife that I was considering that one of them was the killer. What did you do, Nip, with the knife that killed Campero?"

"Put it right there on yore desk—" Wingate said, then stopped abruptly.

Stuart's agate eyes, grown suddenly cold as steel, stared out between the curtains of his narrowed lids. "Then where's it gone?" he said, and there was a new, vibrant quality in his voice that chilled his listeners. "It isn't there now."

Wingate looked and swore.

It was true: there was no knife on the sheriff's desk.

Incredulity stamped the Coroner's sallow countenance. In the sudden silence, unuttered thoughts clamored for words to give them voice. The sheriff's face was stern.

"By cripes!" growled Wingate loudly, "that polecat *has* got nerve!"

Stuart was thinking fast. Plainly, if Wingate had placed the knife on his desk, one of the three men—Tyrone, Bruskell or Broughton—must have taken it, for it was not there now. Which one?

A bitter grin crossed his lips as he asked himself the question. If he knew the answer, he felt, he would know the killer's name!

"Well, I don't believe you'll be able to stop this threatened range war now, Stuart," Allen ventured. "When the news of these three killings gets around, cowmen and sheepmen both will be on the prod. I'm afraid these murders themselves are the start of the range war that's been brewing up around here for the past week. I don't think these crimes are the work of one man."

"There's just one killer in the Cibecue," Stuart's voice was low and even. "Just one killer—a man who loves the silence of a knife!"

Nip Wingate shrugged, relit his pipe and recommenced his puffing.

Allen looked at the sheriff sharply. "You talk as though you knew more than you are letting on. Do you know who this killer is? Do you suspect some particular man?" After a brief pause during which the sheriff said nothing, Allen added:

"Do you think you can nail this killer, Stuart?"

"Yes, I'll get the killer," Stuart said slowly, "and there'll be no range war in Cibecue Valley while I'm wearin' the sheriff's star."

After Wingate and Allen left the office, carrying the body of Caspar Druce to the undertaking parlors in back of Doc Craig's office, the sheriff walked to the open door and stood looking out at the rising sun. Big and red it looked as it peeped above the serrated line of the distant mountain peaks. Big and red and somber.

Stuart watched the rising sun as it changed from red to gold and sent the lowland's purple shadows scurrying to speedy refuge among the distant maze of canyons.

It seemed impossible that so much could have happened in a single night, in the cramped space of a paltry dozen hours. Yet he was aware that in this scanty length of time three men had been murdered, and two lethal attempts had been directed at himself.

What had Dorinda Broughton been doing at the camp at Picture Rock last evening when she had lost her handkerchief? Impatiently he brushed the question aside; he would not doubt Dorinda. No matter what the cause or reason for her having gone there, he could not bring himself to suspect the girl he loved of having had a hand in the sheepman's death.

As he stared into the glowing sky, painted by Old Sol's gaudy brush, Stuart wondered grimly if another dawn would come before the Cibecue killer had forced to a powdersmoke showdown the smouldering, flaring passions that racked the valley.

With a sigh which did not pass his grim, locked lips, the sheriff bent his steps across the road. He strode slowly, alert eyes fixed upon the dusty ground. Back of the second pole corral he found that for which he was looking—the place from which the would-be assassin had slammed that whistling rifle shot. In the dust was the blurred imprint of a recumbent body and an empty cartridge shell ejected from a .30-.30.

For long moments he stood looking down, staring at these signs of the sniper's vigil. Judging by the marks, the man had lain there for some time before his vigilance had resulted in an opportunity to shoot.

"A patient cuss," Stuart spoke the words softly, as though talking to impress the thought upon his mind. "Patient, nervy, cold-blooded and ruthless."

Slipping the spent cartridge shell into one of his pockets, he skirted the corrals and went striding down the street. There was a livery stable in the direction the sheriff was heading, the property of one "Applejack" Smith. It was at this establishment that Stuart kept his horse, and his intention now was to get the animal and ride to the Circle B. Whether he liked the prospect or not, duty demanded that he question Dorinda as to her movements on the night of Druce's death.

13

Striding deliberately, unhurriedly, down the dusty street, Dan Stuart wondered what would happen when the cowmen of Cibecue Valley learned that he, a former cowman and the man they had placed in the Sheriff's Office, had sold his ranch to sheepmen. That naturally he supposed he had been dealing with a cattle syndicate made no difference. He could not tell the cowmen that. Stuart had never formed the habit of explaining his conduct.

Mounted on his big buckskin, Stuart struck out across the range. Tall, broad of shoulder, narrow-hipped, the sheriff rode upright in the saddle, an arresting, masterful figure. And the heavy guns in his sagging holsters looked not one whit more grim and relentless than the tight-pinched line of his determined lips and the cold hard glint in his eyes.

After riding for some time he was amazed to find his thoughts still toying with the personality of Bruskell. Dismissing the man's hard image from his mind he began thinking of Dorinda. Somehow the image which recurred most frequently was the manner in which she had looked at him when she had asked him which side he would back in the event of trouble. He felt certain he had observed a worried light in their clear blue depths.

He recalled how he had thought at the time that Big Cal had put the girl up to asking him those questions. The old cattleman had wished to ascertain in advance which way the cat was going to jump. If the girl had come to him directly from her father, it was instantly evident that her father had not been dead at that time, and must have been speculating about the sheepmen— Why, in the light of Dorinda's question about trouble, it now seemed evident to Stuart that Broughton had known of Druce's death!

As he traversed a timbered draw, the sheriff forgot Dorinda and her father for a time, and his thoughts centered definitely upon Vic Tyrone and the tough bunch who rode for him. An undisciplined, gunslick crew, those riders of the Flying Star, amenable only to the surly will of their hard-drinking boss.

Several ugly tales had reached Stuart's ears anent Tyrone and his hard-riding outfit. It was, however, the sheriff's way to pay but scant attention to rumors, and that only when obviously necessary. When Stuart acted, he preferred to do so on the evidence of his own shrewd eyes.

Nevertheless, he was aware that rumor credited the Flying Star with building too large a loop, and with the wicked habit of carrying surplus cinch rings in their saddle pockets. Illegitimate brandings are often done with cinch rings, so the inference was obvious. Rumor said further that the Flying Star cinch rings were heated whenever opportunity offered—said opportunity taking the form of stray cattle and an isolated canyon.

Bad feeling, as Stuart was aware, had long existed between Tyrone and some of his closest neighbors. It was, he thought, quite possible that this feeling had given impetus to the rumor that the Flying Star was on the make.

As usual, when riding alone across the range, Stuart kept his eyes open and the rifle loose in the scabbard beneath his knee. Despite the fact that weariness claimed him as a result of being in the saddle all day yesterday and being awake all last night, not for an instant did he dare relax his vigilance.

In the Cibecue the price of life was eternal watchfulness, and he who blinked or nodded would be found along the wayside—facedown in the sand or staring up at the stars with glassy eyes.

About him now as the buckskin took him onward lay a sweeping stretch of sand and sage. No tiniest bit of movement, save that created by himself, disturbed the calm serenity of the early morning. But Stuart was taking no chances—it paid to be alert; doubly so if one wore a bit of glinting metal on one's vest!

In an hour or so it would grow insufferably hot out here on the desert's undulating surface. Where now the sand glowed softly, in a short time it would take on a venomous burning glare; its heat would scorch the eyeballs, parch the throat and blister the flesh. Stinging gusts of a capricious breeze would send swirling dust-devils chasing across the silent spaces.

Under the hardy hand of Big Cal Broughton the Circle B had been hewn from the wilderness of sand and stone and sage that was Arizona, and built into a desert kingdom. Old Broughton had never been known to sell an acre of land. Money to him hadn't meant much—but land had been his god. There was one hundred and fifteen thousand acres of owned ground in the feudal estate branding a Circle B. Fifteen keen-eyed, horny-handed riders hung their battered hats in its bunkhouse; fifteen riders drew pay checks once each month.

The ranch had enemies, of course; any outfit that size was bound to have.

Stuart realized full well that one of its enemies might have been responsible for the murder of Cal Broughton; some man he had crossed or tramped on while pulling himself up by his boot straps. Yes, such a solution to the cowman's death was possible, but somehow the sheriff did not think it probable.

As he jogged down the aspen-bordered lane that led to the ranch buildings, he noticed that the bunkhouse appeared empty. No doubt the outfit had already been given its orders by the foreman, pertaining to the day's work, and were off on the business of executing said orders.

Smoke still curled above the tin chimney of the cookshack. Perhaps he was in time to eat with Dorinda. It was a pleasant possibility.

Dorinda appeared on the long veranda that fronted the house. She waved. She was dressed this morning in fringed riding skirt and range boots. The yellow scarf about her neck set off the deep blue of her silk blouse and accentuated the blue of her level eyes.

Stuart swung down from the saddle, racked his horse before the cool veranda, and doffed his hat.

"You're just in time for breakfast, Dan," she greeted.

Her little teeth, seen between her parted lips, were milky like polished rice, but her smile, the sheriff thought, lacked something of its expected warmth.

Her spurred heels jingled pleasantly as she led the way inside. Her blue-black hair, cut long, lay in a rippling cloud about her shapely shoulders.

Stuart, following, felt the delicate charm of her poignantly. Her beauty made a dull pounding in his breast. Beneath his calm exterior he was agitated—why had she not given him her hand or welcomed him more warmly? What, since yesterday, had come between them? But his expression gave nothing of these thoughts away.

The cook placed food upon the kitchen table and they ate with Blinky Evans, the Circle B foreman. The three talked long over their breakfast.

Evans spoke of the probability of coming trouble and Stuart thought sardonically that the threatening range war was surely the basis of every conversation in the Cibecue.

He did not notice what he ate. His mind was on Dorinda. He seemed to sense the mantle of restraint that lay upon her. He wondered again how much she had observed in the camp at Picture Rock.

After Evans had finished and left the room, Stuart leaned forward.

"Druce and his boss herdsman were killed last night."

The faint worried light in the girl's blue eyes grew deeper, otherwise no shade of changing expression crossed her sun-tanned cheeks.

"Have you found who killed them?" Dorinda asked.

"Not yet. I thought perhaps you might have something to tell me."

"I?" She laughed slowly. "What ever gave you such a thought as that, Dan? How would I know anything about it?"

His level gaze regarded her unblinking. "I'm asking you, Dorinda."

Her chin came up. "But why? Why me? I am not acquainted with the sheepmen."

"I thought perhaps you might have been over near Picture Rock last night and might perhaps have seen something."

"I? You thought I might have been near Picture Rock? But why?"

"That, Dorinda, is what I've been wondering."

She regarded him with a level, troubled glance, but did not speak.

"Your father was—" Stuart hesitated, then plunged on; "was killed last night."

The girl's cheeks were suddenly white, the color left her lips. But her beauty, like a steady light, remained. It seemed as though nothing—no shock, however great—could change that. She was taking it like a thoroughbred. Stuart felt a pulse of pride. His statement had been brutal, purposely so. But her reaction was all he could have hoped for. Plainly, she had known nothing of her father's death.

She was speaking now, thickly, as though the words she uttered were rebelling against her will: "I think you had better go now, Dan."

The sheriff rose, face inscrutible, the deep strength of him keeping his features like a mask. With a stiff bow he strode from the room, calm, deliberate. His spurs jingled softly in the silence. Sound ceased abruptly as he reached the veranda.

Nervously Dorinda rose, crossed to a window

and abruptly stopped. As she stood staring out, one hand half rose as though to still the tumult in her breast.

Stuart was standing by the edge of the veranda. He was staring at the horseman who had halted his mount a few feet away. It was Jabe and there was something malignant in his smouldering glance. Slowly he swung from the saddle, a quirt gripped tightly in his right hand.

Advancing to within three feet of the sheriff's motionless figure, he stopped and his gaunt frame bent slightly forward. There was fury in his glance.

"Thought I told yuh my sister didn't want no truck with sheep-lovers!" His yellow teeth gleamed in a sudden snarl. "Didn't I warn yuh to steer clear of the Circle B?"

Stuart's calm face showed no emotion. It was smooth and tranquil and hid his anger well. His clear, deep voice was softly modulated, even:

"I told you to hang around town until after the inquests, Jabe. Why didn't you obey my orders?"

Dorinda, white-faced, watched the scene with mixed feelings. She saw Jabe's high-boned face grow dark and taut; saw his lips writhe back from his yellow teeth. She heard distinctly the hoarse curse that he flung at Stuart; the fighting words, thick with anger, which he hurled across the silence:

"Orders, hell! I ain't takin' orders from you or

any other slat-sided sheep-lovin'—what's so danged low-down that he'll sell his ranch to a bunch of stinkin' sheepmen! I'm gonna give you a quirtin', Stuart, that yuh'll carry to the grave!"

One hushed breathless moment followed. It was ended by the flat, stinging sound of meaty impact as Stuart's driving fist landed flush on Broughton's snarling lips. Jabe reeled backward, caught his balance and stopped. Vile oaths and blood spewed from his battered mouth.

Dorinda watched wide-eyed.

With raised quirt Jabe came charging in, still swearing. He aimed a lashing blow at the sheriff's head and the loaded leather sang through the air in a vicious circle. Stuart stepped back, and the fury with which Jabe had launched his blow swung him half around. Again Stuart struck, and his driving fist brought up against the cowman's head, back of his left ear. As though struck by a pole-ax Jabe went down. Blood seeped out on his jet black hair.

Jabe's gaunt form stretched motionless on the sandy ground. One arm lay limp above his head, the one with the quirt was doubled beneath his body. His feet were wide apart.

Stuart's bronzed face was taut, there was no emotion on it. But his blazing eyes never left Broughton's form till the man rolled over and struggled groggily to his knees. Then he spoke, and his voice was a soft, cold drawl:

"When I give orders, Jabe, I'm used to havin' them obeyed, an' as long as I'm totin' the sheriff's star they're goin' to be. Get on your horse an' hit for town."

He turned, moved to the buckskin standing patiently with dropped reigns and swung aboard. Then he waited, sitting there motionless, until Broughton had hauled himself into his saddle.

When Broughton, with a dark glance of baffled fury, urged his horse down the lane with vicious spurs, Stuart paused for a last look toward the house.

He saw Dorinda at the kitchen window, a hand across her breast. She seemed to be looking at him oddly, then abruptly she turned away.

14

The vast silence of the great dead sea of sand stretched all about him as Stuart rode back toward town. It was hot now—hot with a scorching dryness that chased saliva from the mouth and made the tongue feel like a gob of cotton. A brilliant ball of fiery light blazed relentlessly from the pale blue heavens. Shimmering heat waves danced across the sand and the air seared the lungs like the draft from a furnace.

As the sheriff rode across the burning wastes, carefully conserving the buckskin's strength, he saw before him in the distance from time to time, momentarily skylighted on rolling crest and barren ridge, the fractional blur of a spurring horseman. The rider was Jabe, and he was pushing his mount unmercifully.

As he struck into Cibecue's long main street, Stuart jogged slowly through the hock-deep dust that rose and billowed and spurted at each stroke of the buckskin's hoofs until he reached the front of the Bucket of Blood. There he dismounted and racked his mount.

He stood on the veranda for several moments, staring into the resort across the tops of the swinging doors.

Shorty Glyman was standing beside the bar. He

was engaged in earnest conversation with another man. Stuart was interested in the fellow to whom the stout owner of the 3 Bar 3 was speaking. It was the mysterious, dusty stranger whom he had seen before.

Stuart watched the two men for several moments before turning away. Swinging into the buckskin's saddle he moved down the street toward his office. Since reaching town he had seen no sign of Jabe. Evidently the gaunt cowman was doing his level best to avoid another contact.

Abruptly Stuart pulled his horse to a halt. Nip Wingate was clumping toward him. When the deputy came up with the waiting sheriff, he removed the pipe from his mouth to say: "Yuh heard the latest, yet?"

"I'm not sure. What is the latest?"

"There's a story goin' round that Jabe Broughton's sent outa the Cibecue for a gun fighter to help him solve the sheep problem. If the yarn's true, he's sent for one of the fastest pistol-pushers in the country."

"Who?"

"Cortaro!"

Stuart's agate blue eyes, squinted to keep out the sun glare, refused to reveal emotion. His features as usual were shielded by his mask of calm serenity. His voice, when he spoke, was unhurried:

"Guess we'll have to get to work diggin' up

Bruskell's past, Nip. I ain't sure, but it may be that we can get an angle on this situation through something that happened a long time back. Old hates and feuds die hard here in the desert country; they're passed on from one generation to the next. Who are the old-timers around here who've lived in these parts all their lives?"

"Wal, there ain't many left," Wingate said, dubiously. "There's Applejack Smith. An' ol' Marlano—he lives over near Haystack Butte. An' there's Jake Haskins up to Standard. Reckon that about fills the list. Most of the old fellas in these parts came in later—they wasn't borned here." Wingate looked at his chief, then said: "How about them reward notices? How many do you want printed?"

"Oh, I don't care. Print a bunch of 'em an' see they get scattered around the country. What about Cal Broughton—he was one of the original pioneers around here, wasn't he?"

"He *was*," Wingate answered grimly.

"Uh-huh. Well, it might tie in, you know. You get in touch with Mariano an' Haskins and see what they remember about old feuds Cal Broughton might have been mixed up in. He couldn't have built up a spread like the Circle B without steppin' on somebody's toes. See if any of the authorities in New Mexico have a line on Druce or Bruskell. See if Marlano or old Jake remember a man fitting Druce's description."

"How about Smith?"

"I," Stuart told him softly, "will take care of Applejack Smith."

Wingate turned back toward the office, and the sheriff headed for the livery stable.

The rheumy old eyes of Applejack Smith seemed to scan things in the distant past. Their lids were squinted to protect them from the spiralling smoke of his forgotten cigarettes. There was a faint smile on his parted lips.

"Yeah," he said, at last. "I've lived around these parts all my days, Sheriff. I've known hombres good an' bad—watched 'em come an' go. They only *go,* now. Seems like nobody's interested in settlin' around the Cibecue any more—that is, nobody but Druce an' his sheepmen. I hear you've sold 'em your place near Showlow."

Stuart ignored the hint in Smith's last sentence. He produced a bottle of amber colored liquid from a saddle pocket, uncorked it and handed it to the stableman. Smith threw back his head and tilted the bottle. When he finished, he smacked his lips. "Not bad!" He placed the bottle, the contents of which he had diminished noticeably, on the floor between them. He leaned back against the wall.

"What was you aimin' to find out, Sheriff?"

"You've seen Druce, the sheepman?"

"Yeah, I've seen him. Saw him when he was in town two-three days ago."

"Ever seen him before? Was he here in the old days?"

"Not tuh my knowledge," Smith answered promptly.

"Bruskell ever been around here before?"

"Bruskell? Who's he?"

Stuart explained.

"Nope, I ain't ever seen the gent."

"How about Jabe Broughton? Has he ever been in any serious trouble around these parts?"

The old man's lips curled. "Hell, he ain't been in nothin' *but* trouble so long as I've known him. A surly, vengeful devil if I ever saw one. Don't take a heap after Cal—I guess that ain't hardly to be wondered at, though."

Stuart's penetrating agate glance keened the stableman's face. "How about Cal? Reckon he must have made a heap of enemies while he was buildin' up the Circle B. Any of 'em livin' around here now?"

"I guess he had his enemies—same as every other man that's worth a tinker's dam," Smith said slowly, thoughtfully, in the manner of a man still living in the robust past. "Yeah, he had his enemies, same as the rest of us—but they're about all planted, now. Cal had a habit in the old days of tendin' to such things sort of personal-like an' quick, if you get what I mean. In his younger days, Cal Broughton was a bad hombre tuh monkey with."

"Any of his enemies or their kin still livin' around the Cibecue?"

"Not as I know of. Like I mentioned, Big Cal took care of enemies as they popped up. He didn't let no grass grow under *his* feet. Enemies had a habit of disappearin' quick an' permanent—an' they wasn't put in no lousy jails, neither!"

The sheriff nodded. "There wasn't much law in those days."

"Nope—a man's gun formed the only law." Applejack Smith chuckled. "Cal Broughton's law was plenty potent."

"You used to ride for the Circle B, didn't you?"

"Yeah. I rode for Cal nigh onto twenty year," Smith said, and there was pride in his husky voice. He reached down for the bottle and took a stiff drink. He coughed, wiped his lips and grinned. "We was all fighters in them days, an' Cal was the toughest of us all. A hard fighter an' a hard lover. But Dorinda's maw tamed him down—she had a real calmin' influence on him. . . . She died when Dorinda was born."

"God rest her," Stuart said.

Smith added a solemn "Amen."

A brief hush fell across the odorous stable. A horse stamped restlessly in his stall. Another drove the flies to cover with swishing tail. Smith seemed lost in golden memories; his eyes held a far-away look and there was a gentle smile on his wrinkled face.

"Yep, this was reckless country in the ol' days," he mused. "Fellas settled their diff'rences with fists an' guns. We lived hard an' died the same way. I reckon we all made plenty of mistakes—Cal made one when he married the second time. But shucks, the fellas that don't make mistakes don't never get much out of life. They're afraid tuh live, I reckon. Cal Broughton wasn't ever afraid of anything."

"So Dorinda's mother was Broughton's second wife, eh?" Stuart asked.

"No—Jabe's maw was Cal's second wife. He married Dorinda's maw first. After she died, he moped around four-five years. Then he met Gracie Kelvan—she run a hash house at Holbrook. She didn't live long, neither, after her an' Cal hitched up." The stableman stared at Stuart curiously. "How come you're soundin' me? Why don't yuh take yore questions tuh Cal himself?"

"Cal Broughton," said Stuart quietly, "was murdered last night."

A strained silence, filled with unuttered thoughts, descended on the stable. Stuart stared at the hot sunlight beating in through the open doors, listened to the stamping of the horses and the sporadic buzzing of the flies.

Smith reached down for the bottle, uncorked it and, throwing back his gray head, placed its neck to his wrinkled lips. His Adam's apple bobbed up and down. When the bottle was empty, he threw it in a corner and wiped his lips, drew a sleeve across his sweaty forehead.

"Who did it?" there was menace in his tone.

"I'm trying to find out. Who would you reckon to be the most likely man in these parts?"

Smith's faded eyes filmed over. "Frankly, Sheriff, I couldn't say. Looks like it might be one of them damn sheepmen."

"Druce an' his boss herdsman, Campero, were also murdered last night," Stuart told him bluntly.

"The hell they were!" astonishment stamped the stableman's features. "Guess the range war's started—"

Stuart shook his head. "Sure you can't recall some enemy of Broughton's who is still living in this county?"

"Nope." Smith's tone was firm.

"Can you think of any gent that might be nursin' a grudge against Broughton that doesn't live around here any more?"

Smith's faded eyes scanned the sunlit distance. He remained silent for several minutes.

"No," he said at last.

"You can't think of anyone who'd be glad to see Cal Broughton put out of the way?"

"Sure—plenty."

"But no one that would resort to cold-blooded murder, eh?"

"That's it." Smith turned his faded glance on the sheriff's face. "What makes yuh so sure this ain't the start of the range war everybody's been expectin'?"

"Because it is my notion," Stuart said evenly, "that all three men were killed by the same man."

"Humph!" the stableman seemed thoughtful. "It still might be the start of this sheep an' cattle business. Somebody might have bumped off these men just to get the ball rollin'. Someone who figgered to clean up a profit while the two factions was clawin' at each other's throats."

"I thought of that."

Smith rasped his bristly chin. "What caliber gun was—"

"The victims," said Stuart softly, "wasn't gunned. They was knifed."

15

Dan Stuart sat at the desk in his scantily-furnished office with only the flies to disturb the long run of his roving thoughts. He was tired, weary; his lean-hipped, broad-shouldered body ached in every bone. His curly, yellow hair was wet with sweat. He sat with his square-jawed chin resting in his cupped palms. His face was somber.

What had come between himself and Dorinda? What had he done, or left undone, to disturb their happy relations? Why had she looked at him so oddly there at the kitchen window? And why had she turned away without a parting word?

He caught the clump of booted feet and the rangy jingle of dragging spurs from the board walk outside the office. With an effort he wrenched himself from his somber thoughts and stared at the opening door.

He knew the man who pushed it open, stood there waiting in the hot sunlight gushing in; knew him for a small-spread rancher who ran a brand in the northern part of the valley.

"Come in, Haines. Draw up a chair."

The man came in. He shifted nervously from foot to foot, peering owlishly about the dim-lit office.

"What's on your mind?" Stuart asked. "Speak up."

"It's about them reward notices Wingate's been tackin' up," Haines said, and licked his lips. "Is that straight goods—will you actually pay a thousand bucks for—?"

"Yeah. One thousand dollars will be paid for information leading to the arrest an' conviction of the Cibecue killer," Stuart said. "A fraction of that amount will be paid for information relative to same, accordin' to its worth. If you've got anything to say, let's have it."

"Well, I dunno," Haines seemed dubious. "I been thinkin' it might be Vic Tyrone." He ran a dry tongue across his lips: "I reckon yuh'll keep the sources of yore information secret?"

"So far as is possible," Stuart nodded.

"Well, I heard somebody took a shot at you last night. That right?"

"It is right. Where did you hear about it?"

"Some of the fellas was talkin' about it at the Bucket of Blood a while ago. I jest remembered that I was goin' by here jest a bit before I heard the shot. I seen Tyrone walkin' up this way with a rifle under his arm. He was headin' towards them corrals across the street. . . ."

Stuart looked thoughtful. "Anything else?"

"Hell, ain't that worth somethin'?"

"Might be. Then again it might not. I'll look into it an' let you know."

Haines, about to depart, hesitated. "Uh—I'd rather you didn't mention my name to Vic," he muttered. "He's kind of hot-headed at times, an'—well, I got a wife an' three kids, yuh know. I wouldn't of mentioned this only I'm hard up right now an' need the money bad."

Stuart nodded and Haines went out.

Stuart considered the man's information. So Vic Tyrone had been heading up the street last night, or early this morning rather, with a rifle under his arm. Yes, that needed looking into, all right. Particularly if that had been but a few minutes before someone had shot at him from the shadows of the pole enclosures across the street.

Again he heard the scuffle of boots on the boards outside, and again the office door was pushed open, letting in the hot streaming sunlight, the dust, and a second man. This time the visitor was Glyman, owner of the 3 Bar 3.

Glyman took off his hat and mopped his bald head. When he had replaced his hat he looked at Stuart and scowled malignantly.

"I want to talk to you, Stuart."

"Hop to it."

"Cal Broughton was murdered last night! Why in heck didn't you tell us?"

"I couldn't see any use in spilling that information across the town at a critical time like last night. There was too many cowpokes cashin' their pay checks for liquor. I didn't want to see any trouble get started."

"I'm beginnin' to think you never did want to see any trouble get started," Glyman sneered. "I guess we pulled a boner when we put you in the Sheriff's Office."

"I'm a peace officer," Stuart replied. "I was elected to keep trouble away from this county."

"Like hell, you was! We voted that star tuh you so's we'd have cowman's law in the Cibecue. So that a cowman's rights would get respected; so that—"

"Then you voted it to the wrong man," Stuart cut in coldly. "The law I'm representin' don't take sides."

"No? Well mebbe you won't be representin' it much longer," grunted Glyman, his fat, sweat-beaded face quivering with anger. An ugly grin crept into his pale eyes; "I never did think right smart of fellas that turned their coats!"

There was no flicker of discernible emotion in the sheriff's agate eyes as he rose from his chair behind the desk.

"That kind of talk won't get you anywhere, Glyman."

But Glyman wasn't listening. "There's a story goin' round town today that the Tucumcari Pool yuh sold yore ranch to ain't nothin' but Druce an' his danged sheepmen!" he snarled. "I want to know if that's true."

"Yes, it's true," Stuart's tone was even. "Did you know that Druce was killed last night, too? He was killed before Broughton was. What do you think of that?"

"I think that's fine! If I knew who killed that sheep-raisin' son I'd see that he got a medal!"

"That's dangerous talk at a time like this."

"What the heck do I care? I'm sick of you an' yore pussy-kitten ways! By Gawd, a fella that would sell his cow ranch to a syndicate of sheepmen ought tuh get a rope slapped round his neck!"

"Are you feelin' up to that chore?" came Stuart's cold drawl.

Shorty Glyman's fat bulk abruptly quivered. He forced a shaky laugh that sounded hollow and dismal in the sudden quiet. He backed precipitately toward the door as Stuart strode deliberately forward.

"What—what the heck is eatin' yuh?" Glyman gasped, his fat, sweat-beaded face taking on the color of dried-up clay. "Don't—don't do it, Stuart!"

"That rough talk you been spillin'," Stuart said; "Were those your own notions, or was they read into you by someone else?"

Glyman moistened his heavy lips, but he found speech a sapping effort, "I was told."

The sheriff nodded. "I'd have found it uncommon hard to believe if you'd have claimed them sentiments for your own," he said, then: "Who put you up to this?"

The fat rancher recoiled before the look in Stuart's eyes. He ran his tongue slowly across his lips but seemed unable to find his voice. Queer gurgling noises belched upward from the depths of his throat. The skin on his fat face glistened.

"Was it Jabe Broughton?" Stuart asked.

Glyman's fat bulk swayed and quivered. He glared wildly about the bare office.

"No!" he whispered.

"Was it Vic Tyrone?"

Glyman hesitated, licked his lips. "Yes, it was Vic Tyrone!"

Stuart smiled faintly, seemed about to speak, but held the words back patiently. Spurred boots again were clumping over the boards outside. Glyman stepped hurriedly to one side, out of the hot gush of sunlight. Marshal Obe Shelty swaggered in.

"Sheriff," he said, importantly, "I reckon I can't give you any more co-operation. It's ag'in' my principles to side with sheepherders!"

A sardonic quirk twisted the straight line of Stuart's lips. "So you've got principles, at last. Next thing I know, you'll start breakin' out with religion! I'm goin' to miss your support an' cooperation uncommon bad, Obe. It's tough seein' a friend like you slide out from under."

The marshal's rat-like face went livid at the

sheriff's taunting words. His shrill voice rose in a piping squeak:

"Are you tryin' tuh be funny?"

Stuart shrugged indifferently, turned away. To Glyman he said:

"You better be foggin' along, Shorty. Was I you, I'd pick my friends more careful-like. An' it might not be a bad idea if you'd stuff some cotton in your ears next time you visit the Bucket of Blood. The place seems to have a bad influence on you."

But Marshal Shelty was not to be thrust thus offhandedly aside. "Dang you, Stuart!" he shouted stridently. "I'm talkin' to you an' I expect to be listened at! I say a man what would sell his friends down the river, like you done when yuh sold your spread to them stinkin' sheepmen, ain't no fit man tuh be totin' the sheriff's star!

"It ain't decent! By cripes, I'm a-goin' to see the Board of County Commissioners!"

In three quick strides Stuart crossed to the marshal's glowering figure. Before Shelty realized what was happening, Stuart had swung the smaller man aloft in rigid arms. A moment he held him there, squirming, kicking, swearing. With a saturnine laugh, bitter in its hard-held anger, he flung the marshal out the door. He fell with a muted thud, outsprawled in the heavy dust of Cibecue's street.

"That's a warning, Shelty," Stuart said softly. "Don't come here again."

Glyman stared at the sheriff with bulging eyes. He licked his lips and sidled out the door. When he found the board walk beneath his feet he broke into a lumbering run, his boots sending up spurts of dust at every stride.

Stuart stepped out the door. Deliberately he strode past Shelty where, on hands and knees, with vindictive full-mouthed curses, the marshal was pawing through the yellow dust in search of the gun that had been shaken from his holster.

Untethering his buckskin, Stuart swung to the saddle, sat looking down at the fuming marshal. "You can tell your friends for me," he said with sibilant softness, "that the next man to cast any slurs in my direction had better have his hand on his gun."

16

As he rode out of Cibecue at a comfortable jog-trot, Stuart forgot Obe Shelty and the man's antagonism. He relegated Glyman, Broughton and Blain to distant corners of his mind, and turned his attention on the man he was riding to see—Vic Tyrone, owner of the Flying Star.

For some distance the country through which the sheriff rode was flat; sand, cactus and sage. Sunlight streamed across the waters like a hot and fetid breath. Not a bit of air was moving and the land baked beneath the fiery heat of early afternoon.

Gradually the country grew more broken; bare-ridged hills rose from the desert floor, tangled brush matting their precipitous hollows. The sheriff rode with a loose rein, leaving the question of footing to his mount's good judgment.

After a time his way led through scattered clumps of scrub oak and pinion. Still later, tumbled heaps of granite and upthrust chunks of lava marked the landscape. But Stuart noticed not, or if he noticed, paid scant heed. He was busy with his thoughts, and if they were pleasant, one would never have guessed it, for his brow held furrowed lines and his jaw was grim.

Vic Tyrone was suspected of being a rustler by

some of his closest neighbors, people who were in the best position to know. But suspicion and proof, the sheriff reflected, more often than not lay far apart.

Tyrone was intelligent; he would hide his tracks well. There would be no loose ends for Stuart to get his teeth on. Of this he was assured, for he had known Tyrone for over a year and had come to respect the rancher's ability, although despising his habits and character. Tyrone was no man's fool.

Plainly, it was up to Stuart to track down the unknown killer of Cibecue and see that the man paid the price for his murderous deeds. But equally plain in the sheriff's mind was the need to prevent the range war that was piling up from his carelessness in disposing of his ranch. Yet the two needs seemed not so far apart; indeed, at the moment, they seemed to go hand in hand.

To prevent the threatened range war, he must catch, unmask and punish—or send to punishment—the mysterious knifer who worked so well among the shadows of the night. The man must not be permitted to strike again. The damage he had already done the peace of the valley seemed well-nigh unrepairable.

Was Vic Tyrone the unknown menace?

Having raked his mind the sheriff was forced to admit that the chances seemed highly probable. Yet he was not satisfied. Somewhere, he felt, there was a turn-off he had missed.

Weariness, he mused, was slowing him down. All his faculties did not register. He needed rest; yet doggedly he rode on.

The vast silence of the empty country was soothing to his raw nerves. Gradually, as he rode, his jaw muscles relaxed, the furrows smoothed upon his brow. Yet only for awhile. When the furrows returned, forced outward by his churning thoughts, they were deeper than before; his jutting jaw seemed squarer. His haggard cheeks grew stern.

God, but it was hard to wait! Yet only by waiting, by moving forward warily, could he hope to pin the guilt for these midnight murders where the guilt belonged. He must not permit rash impulses to sway him as he had when a short time ago he had thrown Obe Shelty from his office. Yet it was hard, bitter hard to hold his hand while this storm of abuse was being heaped upon him.

He folded his big hands across the saddle horn, rode with bowed head and hunched forward shoulders through the hot afternoon.

Two hours from Cibecue he sighted the low, weather-whipped buildings of the Flying Star, where they lay slumbering in a tiny sunlit hollow. Huge cottonwoods reared their leafy branches above them, casting welcome shade upon their roofs. Among the trees he saw the whirling blades of a creaking windmill, though there was no breeze where the buckskin moved.

"Sounds like Vic's so full of war thoughts he ain't got time to use an oil can," Stuart said, and smiled faintly when the buckskin's ears flicked forward in agreement.

There were three good-sized pole corrals in the foreground. One of them held several saddle horses, dozing with necks across the bars. The other two were empty and their gates hung bleakly open. The sand-scarred buildings were of adobe. A man sat in the mess-house doorway, puffing on a pipe. Several others lounged in the shade of nearby structures, hats slanted across their eyes, brown-paper cigarettes dangling from their lips.

The ranch house, to one side of the little hollow, was a rambling affair of a single story. The front door was closed and there was no sign of movement behind its windows. Stuart sighed as he caught the general atmosphere: "Seems to be slidin' haywire fast. That's what comes of drink an' war talk, which is Vic's main pastimes lately."

None of the men stirred as Stuart rode into the yard. They lounged where they were and regarded him covertly beneath their down-slanting hat brims. An air of cold and studied hostility struck the sheriff with silent force.

But his face remained calm, indifferent. No twitching muscle conveyed to others the chaotic turmoil of his thoughts, the bitter resentment roused by the punchers' lack of movement.

Three men idled near the hay barn. Stuart

dismounted before them and left the buckskin on dropped reins.

"Vic here?"

The men stared back, but made no immediate answer. Stuart's brow grew dark.

One of the men dropped his hand to gun-butt. Another said:

"He might be in the house."

17

A lumpy couch draped with a bright red blanket occupied one wall of the main room at Flying Star Rancho. Behind the couch, a dirty window looked out upon the huddle of adobe structures decorating the tiny hollow that housed the ranch headquarters. Before the couch stood a small table on which reposed a half-filled bottle of Three Star and a pair of none-too-clean glasses. Upon the couch itself, broad back presented to the window, sat Vic Tyrone.

He was a broad-shouldered, thick-waisted man with slender arms and long-fingered hands. His violent mane of shaggy red hair was mixed with sprinklings of silver at either temple. His little eyes were level but red-rimmed and, taken with the livid scar on his forehead, lent his heavy features an aspect far from pleasing.

His thin lips were twisted in a savage scowl as he sat there on the couch staring morosely at the green bottle on the table. To his way of thinking, he had excellent reason for the scowl. He had been thinking of Jabe Broughton's sister, and had just made an astounding and troublous discovery. He had discovered that he was interested in the girl!

It was truly phenomenal in a man of his temperament. He had never cared for women—

heretofore they had held but a momentary interest for him. But this was different; for weeks now his thoughts had been turning with maddening persistence to Dorinda Broughton. No matter how important the thing of which he was thinking, he would suddenly arouse to find himself beholding in mental vision the image of the graceful Dorinda.

Nor was that all: her glorious charms, reviewed in retrospect, held power to send his blood singing through his veins in thirsty anticipation\ of the time when he should have her for his own.

To be sure, he recognized that she might be in love with another man—possibly with that balky mule of a hated sheriff. But his colossal self-conceit was able to brush Stuart contemptuously aside as a possible rival for her heart and hand. No, Dorinda would cast the sheriff aside without a qualm, he told himself, if she thought she held a chance to hitch up with a man like Vic Tyrone.

It was not the girl that brought the scowl to the rancher's heavy face. It was Stuart. For deep in his soul, Tyrone knew the sheriff would never give the girl up without a fight. And he had no desire for a fight with Dan Stuart.

He wasn't afraid of Stuart, he told himself; hell, no! It was just that Stuart had such a damnably cock-sure way of eying a man. His glance held the power of getting under a man's skin; of making a fellow squirm, no matter how tough he was.

Stuart was a waiter; he couldn't be hurried into anything. He had the patience and hardihood to select his own time for everything. Tyrone could call to mind many occasions in the year he had known the sheriff, in which Stuart had maddeningly out-waited an opponent.

Stuart, as Tyrone well knew, was a man who ultimately would permit no obstacle to stand in the way of a goal he coveted. It might stand for a time, but in the end Stuart would find a way to remove it. The sheriff was a man who would not swerve from a course he set himself, and it was this fact in Tyrone's possession which caused the rancher to scowl. He foresaw trouble, bad trouble, in the near future if he set out to take Dorinda away from the sheriff.

Yet the prospect of probable trouble for himself did not lessen Tyrone's resolve to win Dorinda for himself. He would have her, come what might.

He must find some way to remove the hated sheriff from his path. He thought of several ingenious ways, but soon discarded them all. Dan Stuart must be removed permanently. In his case, no half measures would bring the desired result.

The more Tyrone thought of Stuart, the more savage became his scowl.

He poured himself a stiff three fingers of the green bottle's content, but felt no better.

Stuart's confidence, efficiency and calm

assurance had been stumbling blocks on which a number of men had broken their necks. Vic Tyrone's must not be broken thus. And yet to out-wait the sheriff required a patience far in excess of that possessed by Tyrone, as the rancher freely admitted. He must ally circumstances to his cause if he wished to beat Dan Stuart.

And favorable circumstances, he reflected, were already hard at work to break the sheriff. The very stubborn, unbending will which was Stuart's greatest asset, Tyrone decided, would sooner or later prove the man's undoing. The cowmen were steadily turning against him because of his unswerving stand on this sheep and cattle issue. Very well; he would use his strength and cunning to turn them further.

He smiled at the thought, but the smile quickly faded as he recalled the humiliation he had already suffered at the sheriff's hands.

He swore viciously as he recalled how the sheriff had made him take water before his fellow cowmen in the Bucket of Blood the night before. And again in the shadowed yard behind the resort, directly after. And still again in the Sheriff's Office before Nip Wingate, in the ink-black hours of early morning.

"Curse his soul, he'll pay dear for that before I'm through with him!" Tyrone swore, rising from his seat to stride restlessly up and down the floor. And at each stride of his muscular body, the pointed rowels on his glittering spurs clinked angrily, like a rattler's buttons.

"A tough gun, dang his hide, but I'll head him hellward yet!"

He thought of the gun fighter Broughton was importing, and felt a bit comforted. The man might be hired to use his guns against Dan Stuart. He would have to see. It depended on the fellow's character, more than on the speed of his hands, he thought.

In the meantime, Tyrone decided, he would have to be extremely careful lest some careless word or action should set Stuart on his trail. He shivered slightly at the thought of Stuart hunting him.

"Cripes!" he muttered, and, tilting the green bottle to his lips he drank till the thing was empty. Then he hurled it into a corner and wiped his lips with a savage gesture.

Some sixth sense or premonition drew his glance abruptly to the window. His muscular frame went rigid as, staring out, he swore. Dan Stuart, astride his buckskin, was even now swinging into the hollow.

He did not stop to reason, but prepared himself for trouble. His right hand dropped to the heavy pistol swinging in scarred holster at his thigh. He took it out and examined it carefully, after which he ejected the cartridges and replaced them with fresh ones from his belt. Then, pouching it, he strode to the door.

But thinking better of the impulse, he backed away. If Dan Stuart wanted him, let him come to the house. He took up a position in the middle of the floor, beside a table stacked with old magazines and newspapers, and waited, right thumb hooked in his gunbelt not far from the holstered .45. His nostrils quivered, and the red-rimmed eyes above them narrowed until they were mere slits of frosty light.

"Step in," Tyrone growled, in answer to the knock upon the door. Speaking, he bent forward slightly from the waist.

The door opened and Dan Stuart stood there facing him. "Howdy, Vic," he said.

"Come in an' shut the door," muttered Tyrone gruffly. And when the sheriff had done so, never taking his eyes from Tyrone's rigid form, the rancher asked:

"What brings you out this way in the middle of a hot afternoon?"

"I was ridin'," Stuart said vaguely, "an' thought I might as well stop in an' pass the time of day. Sure is hot."

"Yeah," Tyrone grinned faintly. "Sorry I can't offer yuh a drink, Stuart. But I seldom drink at home an' never keep liquor in the house. Creates a bad example for the cowpokes. Like you told me las' night, a fella can't be too careful these days."

"That's right," Stuart nodded. "I hear Jabe

Broughton has sent out of the valley for a gun slinger. Heard anything about it, Vic?"

"Oh, I heard some palaver in the Bucket of Blood last night to that effect. But I didn't take much stock in it—don't now, either. Just some of Jabe's cheap talk, I reckon likely. He knows, like the rest of us, that you don't want no sheep an' cattle trouble in the Cibecue. I don't think, under the circumstances, Jabe would be makin' a o-vert move like sendin' for a gun fighter."

"Well, I'm glad to hear it," Stuart said, then asked:

"What do you make of this Bruskell hombre? I guess you've seen him?"

"Oh, yeah," Tyrone grinned dryly, "I've seen him, all right. Tough fella. He has a mean eye. Like old Druce had," he added reminiscently. "If I was you, Stuart, I'd be real careful if I was gonna do any solo ridin' around this country like you are doin'. Some gent with a loose conscience might try tuh pot you from the brush. This unknown killer we got in the Cibecue, mebbe."

Try as he would and did, Tyrone was unable to detect any change in Stuart's features resulting from his pointed remark. It was exasperating; the man had a face that was about as mobile as a sandstone crag, he thought bitterly. Stuart's ability to mask his feelings was a never-ending source of irritation to the muscular owner of the Flying Star.

"Thanks, Vic. I'm keepin' my eyes open," Stuart

said, with a faint smile the rancher did not like. "If some gent of easy conscience should so far forget himself as to take a crack at me, like you suggest, he'd better make sure his first shot does the trick. I don't aim to be caught napping, again. But I don't guess there's much danger of that. The fellow is someone whom we all know, I should imagine. Some gentleman who prefers the silence of a knife. Perhaps you've noticed?"

"Who, me?" Tyrone forced a look of bland surprise to his countenance. "No, I ain't noticed. Heck, the gent an' me ain't never been introduced! You got any notion who he is?"

Stuart evaded the question. Instead, he asked one of his own:

"Reckon it was kind of cold out there by the corrals this mornin', wasn't it, Vic?" and his glance dropped casually to the rancher's .30-.30 rifle that was standing in a corner of the room.

Tyrone took a firm grip on himself. He started to speak, but found that his voice was not in the iron control he thought, and stopped. He modulated his voice with a physical effort that blanched his face a trifle.

"I don't get this, Stuart," he said with evident bewilderment. "What c'rrals are you talkin' about?"

"The pole enclosures across the street from my office, Vic."

"I can't see what they've got tuh do with me.

How in hell would I know whether it was cold out there this mornin'? That's a hell of a question to ask me. What give yuh that notion, Stuart? Yuh don't think I've been hangin' around them damn corrals, do yuh?"

"I was wondering," the sheriff said softly.

Tyrone felt his frame growing rigid again. His right hand was still hooked by its thumb to his gunbelt, and he kept it there, moving it a trifle closer to his holstered weapon. He laid his eyes on Stuart in a truculent stare:

"What are you tryin' tuh frame up on me, fella?"

"Not a thing, Vic. I was just wondering," Stuart repeated.

"Yeah? Well, you're wastin' your time, then. I got all I can do to run this cow spread without spendin' my nights hangin' out around them cussed c'rrals across from your Cibecue office. You got any more crazy notions in your head?"

"A few, Vic. Just a few. For instance, when was the last time you used this .30-.30 in the corner?"

Tyrone's features took on a frankly puzzled look. "Shucks, I dunno. Eight or ten days ago, mebbe. What the heck are you drivin' at, Stuart?"

"Someone," said Stuart softly, "lay over by them pole corrals last night or early this morning an' took a shot at me with a .30-.30 rifle."

Tyrone felt the hair bristle on his neck. His hand moved closer to the smooth black butt of the gun on his thigh. "Are you accusin' me, Sheriff?"

Stuart shook his head. "I'm not accusin' anyone, Vic. You asked me what I was drivin' at an' I gave it to you straight."

"Well, yuh needn't think I was parked out there in the dark an' dew just to get an added edge I wouldn't noways need," Tyrone growled angrily. "Heck, if I wanted tuh see you planted, Stuart, I'd—"

"Sure, I know, Vic. You'd come right up to me as man to man and say 'Stuart, I don't like your looks. Haul your guns or get out of town.' "

Tyrone stared with slitted eyes, waiting for a smile to break on Stuart's lips. If Stuart smiled, he told himself, there'd be powder smoke fogging the air the next instant if it cost him his life.

But Stuart did not smile. Nor did his maddening calm self-confidence desert him for a second. He nodded slowly, and his cold unblinking gaze, unfathomable as agate, did not leave Tyrone's.

"I'll be jogging along now, Vic," he said. "I want to be back in town by grub time. Got to keep an eye on things, you know. Can't have these hotheaded cowmen stirring up trouble. Got enough trouble now. Well, so long, Vic."

Tyrone relaxed. "So long."

The sheriff turned his broad back, walked deliberately to the door, opened it and, stepping out into the hot sunlight, closed it behind him.

Vic Tyrone let out a soft-voiced curse. "Tough as mesquit, dang him!"

• • •

When Stuart had ridden away, Tyrone paced restlessly up and down the room for some while. From time to time his big fists clenched and a cloudy light crossed his red-rimmed eyes. Once he spoke aloud, showing the trend of his thoughts:

"He's a tough hombre all right, an' he's hard as nails, dang him! But tombstones is powerful easy sproutin' in the Cibecue. An' there'll be one shovin' up for him, before long."

After a time he flung himself on the blanket-draped couch, but almost immediately he was up again and striding toward the door.

He flung it open and hurled a loud bellow across the yard:

"Shane!"

One of the men sitting before the bunkhouse, a tall saturnine fellow, slouched to his feet and came jingling across the uneven ground to the ranch house door.

"Yeah?"

"You an' a coupla the boys get that herd of scrub cattle yuh gathered up on the move toward Spotted Mountain. Keep 'em outa the foothills, an' when yuh reach Spotted Mountain bed 'em down an' ride circle on 'em. A couple of Broughton's boys'll be hazin' along some more longhorns some time tonight an' will turn 'em in with ours. Blain may send some, too. Hold everything until yuh get word from me."

"You gonna be along?"

"Mebbe so, mebbe not—accordin' to the way the hands is dealt. Probably I will, though. I'm goin' over to the Circle B now. We're makin' medicine there tonight." Tyrone grinned and gave the man a wink.

Shane grinned back. "Anything else?"

"No. Get goin'."

"What if we should bump into the sheriff? He'll be some curious about a night drive, won't he?"

"I shouldn't wonder but what he would, if he was to see it. But he won't. He's gone back to Cibecue. Get them cattle started, an' don't pick any daisies on the way tuh Spotted Mountain."

"Okeh by me, boss," Shane grunted, and went jingling back across the yard. Two of the men idling near the hay barn rose and moved to join him. Shane said something in a guarded voice. The three turned and went clumping toward the corral with the closed gate. They got ropes from their saddles and shook them out.

Several minutes later, three horses had been snaked from the enclosure. The men were busy slapping their gear upon the mustangs' backs. A few moments later Tyrone saw the three punchers mount and go loping out of the hollow.

Grinning, as at some secret joke, the rancher strode toward the corral himself, and shaking out his rope, caught himself a big blue gelding, which he made short work of saddling.

One hour, to the minute, after Stuart had left the Flying Star to return to Cibecue, Vic Tyrone, mounted on the blue gelding whose long legs promised speed, left the buildings of his ranch behind.

After a short ride he struck a road which he followed to Murdock. There he stopped for supper. He hardly noticed the smiling waitress who gave him great attention, for his thoughts were at the Circle B, where he hoped to find himself shortly after dark.

After washing down a hurried supper with a steaming cup of black coffee, Tyrone left the restaurant. Settling into the saddle, he swung the blue gelding on along the road at a smart trot which, after a time, he increased to a gallop. He stayed with the road until it crossed Carrizo Creek, then left it to strike eastward across the range in the direction of Broughton's Circle B.

He cantered into the ranch yard an hour after dark. One of the Circle B hands came up to take his horse. Swinging from the saddle, Tyrone threw the man the reins, and with his springy muscular stride crossed to the foreman's shanty.

Evans was sitting on the doorstep, smoking. "Guess yuh heard about Cal gettin' rubbed out last night?" he asked without preamble.

"Yeah," Evans said. "I heard, Mister."

Tyrone stared through the darkness. "You don't like me a awful lot, do you?"

"Well, I don't know as I'd wanta kiss yuh," Evans said drily.

"Humph! You better watch yore tongue, Evans. Things is gonna be different around here now. Jabe's the dawg with the brass collar in this outfit, now."

"Yeah, I reckon that's so."

"Well, Jabe's a good friend of mine, Evans." Tyrone paused, then added:

"Dorinda, too."

"Jabe never did exercise good judgment, tuh my way o' thinkin'," yawned the foreman frankly.

Tyrone snorted, was about to turn away, then stopped.

"Anyone got here, yet?"

"I don't know. Who are you expectin'?"

"Blain and Obe Shelty ought to be showing up here tonight. Glyman, too. Then there's another fella, Cortaro, who Jabe's expectin' to drop in."

"Well, none of them gents has showed so far," Evans answered. "Far as that goes, I reckon the scenery will be better off without bein' decorated with most of them gents."

"You're kinda salty for an old rooster, Evans. You better tone that talk down if you're expectin' to stay on here. When me an' Dorinda get hitched up—"

"What you been smokin', fella?"

"Huh?"

"You talk," Evans answered, "like yuh might

have been mixin' some of that there loco weed with your tobacco. I hadn't heard that Dorinda was thinking of gettin' hitched up to anybody. An' if she is aimin' to, I reckon she knows where she can find a gent more to her likin'."

Tyrone stepped close to the old foreman, tapped him on the chest with a long trigger-finger:

"That'll be enough outa you, fella. Another crack like that an' I'll close your mouth fer keeps!"

"It's a free country," Evans said defiantly.

"That depends on whether a fella has good sense or not," Tyrone grunted softly, and without further words, strode across the clearing toward the ranch house door.

18

Navajo County provides for its Sheriff's use an automobile.

Returning from Standard in this machine, which Stuart had driven down from Holbrook, Nip Wingate sat puffing his battered pipe and meditating on the futility of his efforts to secure information. To his way of thinking, he had learned less than nothing during his talk with old Jake Haskins. The man was becoming childish. The whole business, Nip Wingate told himself frowningly, was a downright waste of time.

Before setting out for Standard, he had made an attempt to visit old Morales, who lived near Haystack Butte, down in the next county to the south. But upon reaching the Salt River, he had found the bridge under process of repair or reconstruction. To save him, he could not have decided which. But at any rate, he had been unable to cross. A workman had told him that it would be useless to cross the stream, even if the bridge had been in condition for such a crossing, since the road beyond was closed to travel indefinitely. There was no way, he said, of getting near Haystack Butte by car.

Swinging into Cibecue's dusty street, the deputy brought his machine to an abrupt and squealing stop. Climbing out before the Sheriff's Office, he found the place deserted.

Then, realizing that he had accumulated considerable alkali during his dizzy trip up and down the country, he ambled toward the Bucket of Blood with the laudable intention of irrigating his system.

But, reaching the resort and entering, he stopped abruptly just inside its swinging doors. There were not more than six or eight men inside the place, mostly townsmen. Yet an air of great excitement hung over the long room. Everyone seemed to be talking at once. Plainly, thought Wingate, something notable had happened.

Striding to the bar, he rapped a coin upon its surface—with no result. He rapped again, impatiently. The bartender said, without turning his head:

"Hold your horses, fella. I'll be with yuh in a minute."

"A minute's too dang long tuh wait!" Wingate snapped. "I'm in a hurry."

Recognizing the unwelcome voice of Authority, the bartender turned and, seeing the identity of his impatient customer, moved reluctantly down the bar.

"What'n heck's the matter with them fellas?" Wingate demanded testily, indicating the group of townsmen to whom the bartender had been listening. "Tuh hear 'em jabber, a gent would think this was a family reunion, or somethin'."

"Hmm. Well," said the barman, rolling up his sleeves, and leaning forward as though about to confide a great secret, "this here's somethin' of a red-letter day in the history of Cibecue. Do you know who's in town?"

"It must be the president of these United States, at least, judgin' by the commotion them fellas is makin'," Wingate commented drily.

"Shucks, no. It's Cortaro!"

"An' yuh mean tuh say they're makin' all that stew over a measly gun fighter!"

"Measly! Gosh, Cortaro's one of the greatest gun slingers in the whole southwest!"

"That don't make him no better in my estimation," said Wingate, flatly. "Gun fighters, tuh my old-fashioned way o' thinkin', ain't nawthin' but poison insects, like rattlesnakes an' scorpions an' Gila Monsters. A professional gun fighter, Mister, is a man what takes money for bumpin' off unfortunate gents what ain't as quick on the trigger as himself, or shoots in the back them that are!"

"My gosh, Nip, you better not let him hear you say that!"

"I'd as soon tell him to his face," said Wingate testily, moving to the doors, his drink forgotten. "Mebbe I will, if I see him."

"Hey, wait a minute!" the barman said. "You better put two or three drinks under your belt if you're aimin' to hunt trouble with Cortaro." As Wingate returned to the bar, he added:

"You heard about Stuart chuckin' Obe Shelty out of the Sheriff's Office, this noon?"

"Huh!" Wingate looked startled. "Well, that *is* news! Tell me about it."

As the loquacious bartender proceeded to do so, Wingate began to feel his old loyalty and trust come creeping back into his veins. Maybe he had been underestimating the sheriff, after all. Perhaps it wasn't fear that stayed his hand under the tide of abuse being heaped upon him by public opinion. Perhaps he was moving cautiously for quite another reason. Perhaps—

"Well, I gotta be goin'," he said aloud, and downed his drink. Picking up his change, he headed for the doors again. He stopped when he reached them and called back over his shoulder:

"I don't reckon Obe Shelty's spreadin' that adventure o' his around town. Who told yuh?"

"Shorty Glyman was there when it happened."

"Oh, I see," and with a puzzled look, the deputy left the resort.

As Nip Wingate clumped his way along the board walk that led to the Sheriff's Office, he was busily whittling shavings of tobacco off his chunk of Brown's Mule. When he had accumulated a considerable quantity, he put his knife and the remainder of the plug away and stuffed the shavings in the blackened bowl of his old pipe. Striking a match, he lighted the concoction without faltering in his stride, and inhaled gratefully.

"Nothin' like the solace of good tobacco in troublous times," he muttered, and clumped on up the street.

As he reached the general store, its proprietor, who had observed his coming, stuck his head out the door and beckoned furtively. Wingate swung from his measured course and entered the store, finding no one in its interior but the proprietor.

"Well, Margate, what's up?"

"Shh!" the storekeeper cautioned. "Come over here by the counter."

When Wingate had followed the man as requested, Margate pointed to a box of knives that lay among a litter of other things. "Look at that!" he muttered, pointing.

With a puzzled expression, the deputy studied the box. "Wal?"

"Wal! My Gawd, Wingate! Look at 'em!"

The deputy puffed hard at his pipe. "I'm lookin', Margate, but all I see is a box o' knives. What's wrong with 'em? They dull, or somethin'?"

"*Dull!* Land o' Tophet!" muttered Margate, as though exasperated. "The Lord knows what Stuart ever made *you* a depity for! *Dull!* Oh, Lord; count 'em!"

The deputy did so, puffing complacently the while. "Fifteen, I make it."

"Yeah," snapped Margate. "Fifteen. Last night when I locked up at seven o'clock, there was twenty-one there—"

"How do yuh know there was?"

"How do I know? My Gawd, don't I run this store?"

"Wal, I reckon. Anything else?" asked Wingate, looking around.

"Y'betcha! Take a look at the back window there!"

Wingate strode to the window in question and examined it perfunctorily. "Uh-huh," he said, squinting. He puffed some more, seeming to scan several things in his mind. Then he looked at the storekeeper. "Kinda looks," he said slowly, "like somebody might have busted in here las' night."

"Yeah," drily, "it does kinda look that way." Arms akimbo, Margate stared the deputy in the eye. "Some damn rascal has hooked six of my new knives!"

"Sho," Wingate's tone was meant to be soothing. "Don't get het up about it. He might have taken more."

"I wanta know what you're going to do about it."

"About what? The knives? Or the fella what took 'em?"

"Both!" the storekeeper exploded with an oath.

"Why, I reckon I'll have to tell the sheriff about it," Wingate said. "I expect he'll be sort of interested."

"Yes, I shouldn't wonder but what he will. Don't you realize the significance of this theft?"

"Why, sure," Wingate grinned around his pipe. "There's a robber loose in Cibecue."

Margate stared and shook his head. "Solid ivory," he muttered.

"Listen," said Wingate softly, tapping the storekeeper's chest with his pipe-stem; "you're thinkin' that the feller what stole them knives is the Cibecue killer. You're thinkin' that he killed the victims with your knives. An' between ourselves, I expect you're right. But the sheriff won't want this news tuh be gettin' round. Was I you, Margate, I'd keep my lip buttoned tight about this."

"D'you think I'm a fool?"

"Wal, you will be if yuh tell this story to anybody else," the deputy grunted. "I'm gonna look around an' see can I find some gent what saw some other gent crawlin' in your back window last night."

As Nip Wingate, followed by another man, approached the Sheriff's Office half an hour later, he saw Stuart's buckskin tethered to the rail in front. "Stuart's back," he grunted. "Let's step on it."

As they entered the office, Wingate saw at a glance that the place was empty.

"You wait here," he told his companion. "Stuart's probably down at the restaurant, gettin' a bite to eat. Stick around here till I fetch him back."

As rapidly as possible, Wingate covered the distance between the office and the restaurant. He did not run because he had no wish to attract attention. Nevertheless, he made good time, and found Stuart as he had expected. The sheriff was just reaching for his hat.

When Stuart had joined him outside, Wingate said in a guarded voice:

"Let's get up to the office quick. I got a fella there you'll wanta talk to, I shouldn't wonder."

"What about?" Stuart asked, swinging into step.

"There was a robbery at the general store last night. Some thievin' son stole six of Margate's new Bowies."

Stuart nodded, eyes bright with interest. "This fellow thinks he knows who stole 'em, eh?"

"He's got an idea," Wingate said, and proceeded to tell the sheriff of his trip to Standard, and the scant results thereof. "Haskins is gettin' silly—plain downright daffy," he wound up. "Told me that Jabe Broughton wa'n't Big Cal's son! Can yuh imagine such fool talk as that? Cripes! I reckon ol' Jake's about ready fer plantin'."

"What," asked Stuart, "did he say about Druce an' Bruskell? Did he remember anyone answerin' to their descriptions?"

"Said he recalled a gent back in the seventies

that mighta been Druce—a fella called 'Dud-Eye' Gale." Wingate snorted. "I tell yuh the ol' coot's in his third childhood. When I came up to his shack he called me Sherman, an' stuck a border rifle in my belly. Cripes, I thought fer a minute the dang fool would shoot me!"

They strode several paces in silence, then Stuart asked:

"What about Marlano? Did you see him?"

"No," Wingate muttered. "I got as far as the Salt an' found the durn bridge torn up. A fella workin' on it told me that the road was closed beyond. We'll have tuh do without any help from Marlano. Anyway," he added, sardonically, "if he's got as feeble in the head as Jake Haskins, I reckon we ain't out much if we don't get tuh palaver with him!"

Dusk had been settling rapidly when the two lawmen left the restaurant. By the time they reached the Sheriff's Office, the vast, impenetrable cloak of night had fallen across the town, through which the lights of dwellings twinkled with the effect of diamonds in an ebony crown.

No lamp illuminated the office. Just outside, Wingate placed his hand on Stuart's arm. "I forgot tuh tell you," he said, "that Cortaro has done arrived in this metropolis."

Silent, Stuart led the way into the office. Fumbling in his pocket for a match, he heard Wingate call:

174

"Haines!"

But there was no answer from the darkened room.

The sheriff struck his match. Nip Wingate let out a curse.

19

Revealed in its every nook and corner by the light of the sheriff's flickering match, the scantily-furnished office was devoid of human occupation. There was no sign of Haines. Nor could they find any sign of his having been there.

Expelling his breath in a soft sigh, Stuart lit the lamp that was bracketed to the wall.

"Gone!" swore Wingate, frowning.

"Pulled out," decided the sheriff.

"Yuh mean he left here purposely? But why? What would he want to do that for?"

"I guess he got to thinking things over after you left him here alone."

"I still don't get the picture," Wingate muttered, scowling.

Stuart dropped wearily onto one of the bunks and closed his eyes. "Haines probably got to thinking and decided that cold feet might be the better part of valor. If the killer thought Haines suspected him, and saw Haines coming toward my office or waiting around in my office, Haines' life wouldn't be worth two wags of a cow's tail. Probably Haines had the fact occur to him an' got scared out."

"Oh. I was kinda thinkin' mebbe Vic Tyrone was the gent we was after," Wingate ventured.

"Vic Tyrone might be in town. Or Haines might think Vic was in town. Haines gave me some information this morning about Vic."

"He did?"

"He told me that he'd heard somebody took a shot at me just before daylight. He said he'd heard the shot. And just before he heard it, Vic passed him headin' this way an' carryin' a rifle."

Wingate stared, but the sheriff's eyes were still closed. His face was beginning to show the strain Stuart was under from lack of sleep. There were new lines in it Wingate had not observed before.

"Uh-huh," Wingate said, nodding to himself. "I guess you been out to the Flyin' Star this afternoon."

"Yeah."

"Did yuh see Vic's rifle?"

"I saw it—a .30-.30."

"What caliber rifle was the shot fired from that broke our clock?" Wingate asked.

Stuart put a hand in his pocket, then held the hand out. In its open palm lay the shell he had picked up from the dust around the corrals that morning.

Nip Wingate whistled softly.

"What you've got to do," said Stuart, slowly, "is to get hold of Vic's rifle somehow an' fire it."

"What for? An' why me?"

"Because you'll have a better chance than I will. The chances are Vic won't be usin' that rifle for a while. He'll be usin' one of his others," Stuart explained.

"Yeah, but what do we want to fire his .30-.30 for?"

"You need a rest, too, Nip. You ain't thinkin' right. I want that rifle fired so I can compare the pin marks on shell with this shell I picked up by the corrals."

"Then yuh think Vic is our man, eh?"

"I don't know. I'm reservin' judgment. Who did Haines say he saw?"

"He didn't say," Wingate answered drily. "He was waitin' to tell you."

"Uh-huh. Let me sleep for about an hour, Nip, then wake me up. I want to look this Cortaro hombre over. But right now I got to sleep. . . ."

The sheriff's tired voice trailed off. He was asleep before he finished speaking.

An hour later Wingate woke him up. He made several futile attempts before he finally succeeded in rousing Stuart to realization of his surroundings. Stuart growled: "I bet I could sleep thirty-six hours an' never know it."

Rubbing his eyes he rose from the bunk and went outside. Wingate heard him splashing his head in the horse trough.

"I'm feelin' more awake, now," he said with a wry grin, as he re-entered the office. "But I'm still kinda short in the temper."

"Yeah, I reckon. I ain't feelin' so cheerful myself," Wingate answered. "What are yuh figgerin' tuh do?"

"Reckon I better go take a peek at this hired killer; I've heard a deal about him durin' the last couple years. He's got quite a reputation as a lead-dispenser, 'cording to what folks tell me."

"Yeah, an' the bigger the rep, the easier it is for some smart gent tuh drop 'em," Wingate snarled. "These gun-slicks go along cautious as all heck till they get themselves a rep. Then they sort of get to feelin' like they can't be beat. They get careless an' soft. Along comes another gent with a similar load o' speed an' a hankerin' to get the killer's kudos. Comes a puff o' smoke, a burst o' flame, an' there lays Mister Killer in the dust.

"There's not many of these gun fighters left," he added grimly, "but if I had *my* way, I'd corral the lot of 'em an' stand 'em up ag'in' a 'dobe wall!"

Stuart put on his hat, pulled its brim down low across his eyes. "I reckon you would, at that," he grinned.

"Durn right, I would. What about them inquests we was s'posed to have today?"

"I got the Coroner to postpone 'em a while," Stuart answered. "Figured it might be just as well to wait a bit. I'll admit it's kinda hot, but I expect to have this knifer under lock an' key inside another day." He stepped out into the velvet black

179

of the night. The moon was sleeping overtime, it had not yet got up.

Wingate listened to the diminishing clump of his boots along the boards of the walk, and the pleasant jingling of his spur chains. When the sounds had faded out, he shook his head and commenced refilling his battered pipe.

"A square-shooter, that gent," he muttered softly. "I don't quite get the idee of him sellin' the S Bar 4 tuh Druce an' his amigos, but I'm here tuh say that it takes an uncommon amount of guts to sell your ranch to a bunch of sheepmen, an' make the cowmen like it. I'm for him—even if I ain't so dang partial to his stand in this range feud that's boilin' up!"

When the young sheriff of Navajo County entered the Bucket of Blood Saloon at a quarter of nine by the fly-speckled clock on the wall above the bar, he sensed at once that indescribable atmosphere that follows on the heels of violence. Even had his nostrils not caught the fading taint of gun smoke, he would have known by the rigid postures of the assembled patrons that Death had recently made itself manifest.

There were hardly more than a dozen men in the resort he saw, as his probing glance raked the room. Five of this number were grouped about a faro table at the rear, where they stood like statues, their hard taut faces mobile as so many chunks of wood. The others, all but two, and with faces equally void of expression, were ranged along the bar.

Of the two exceptions, one lay on the floor in a prostrate heap, pitifully still and desolate in the garish light of the coal-oil lamps. The other stood in a graceful yet sinister slouch above him, bright hawk-like eyes sweeping the room with a derisive glint. It was on this latter that all attention seemed to be fixed.

In a cold, bloodless way, the man had a handsome face. It was handsome despite the tight, thin mouth, waxed mustache and hawk-like eyes. It was framed in a huge bell-crowned sombrero looped to his chin with a scarlet cord. A tight-fitting dark velvet jacket set off his pale blue shirt, a yellow scarf was pulled tight about his throat, Mexican chaps covered his leg-clutching trousers of blue corduroy. Though faded and scarred by long usage, studdings of silver and turquoise gave frank evidence of their worth.

A braided quirt hung from his left wrist; his right lay against the cartridge belt that sagged at his groin with the weight of the big pistol that reposed in the brass-studded holster with open top.

Dan Stuart realized as soon as he saw him that this was the famed Cortaro. And, if appearances were any criterion, he thought it equally plain that already the man had been practising his trade.

A breathless silence, tense and brittle with

unspoken thoughts, hung over the room as the sheriff paused inside the swinging doors. No man's eyes swung toward him; all were concentrated on Cortaro, where he stood above his victim.

Suddenly the gun fighter grinned—a saturnine grimace which he distributed impartially among the watching townsmen. One after another they looked hurriedly away.

"Self defense, eh, amigo?" his hawk-like eyes picked out the countenance of Klinn, proprietor of the resort, where he stood beside the bar.

Klinn blinked his sleepy eyes rapidly, gulped. "Yeah," he spoke with effort, "that's right. Self defense."

"This paisano," gently the gun fighter prodded the man on the floor with the toe of one dusty boot, "he drew the gun first, no?"

Klinn wet his lips nervously. "Yeah—that's right."

"You hombres," Cortaro's piercing glance swept Klinn's patrons, "ain't holdin' out any doubts, are yuh?"

As a single unit the townsmen shook their heads.

"That's fine," Cortaro laughed, smoothly, easily. "If a couple of you strong gents'll carry out the late deceased, I'll set up the drinks." He looked at Klinn: "Tres dedos each—to our better acquaintance, señors."

Klinn moved behind the bar himself, set bottles and glasses along its top. The patrons crowded forward with alacrity. If there were any among them who mourned the passing of Cortaro's victim, they wisely kept the fact to themselves.

Stuart moved away from the doors and leaned against the wall. If Cortaro noticed him, he paid no attention.

After the drinks were downed, Klinn set them up on the house. "That makes twice," thought Stuart ironically, for the gun fighter had produced no money for his treat. Apparently Colonel Colt had *not* made all men equal.

After a time the gambling element of the crowd returned to the faro table at the rear of the room. Talk was desultory. In the silence the slap of cards, the clink of coins and the tinkle of glasses could be plainly heard, and occasionally the restless *clump* of stirring boots.

Stuart stood where he was, idly watching the throng. Several men had noticed him and nodded. The sheriff had returned their nods but had not spoken. He was waiting. . . .

Less than fifteen minutes had elapsed since he had entered the place when the swinging doors parted and a Circle B puncher came jingling in with flapping chaps. He sent a hasty glance about the room, a glance that lingered momentarily on the smiling gun fighter, then went to the worried features of Pecos Klinn.

He crossed the room, stood lounging against the bar and said something in an undertone to the saloon keeper. Klinn nodded toward Cortaro. The puncher turned and studied the gun fighter cautiously. Then he crossed to the man's side and handed him a note.

Cortaro's hawk-like gaze flashed hurriedly across the paper, then up at the watching puncher. He smiled lazily.

"All right, amigo," he said and, making many little pieces out of the big one, dropped the paper to the floor. "Le's ride."

But as the puncher led the way to the door, Cortaro's wary eyes caught those of Stuart and he swerved aside.

"El Señor Tinbadge?" He looked the sheriff insolently up and down. "How does it happen, amigo, you have not extended me the glad welcome, eh?"

The calm tranquillity of Stuart's glance held squarely the other's gaze. "You haven't come to the right place, that's all. I welcome gun fighters at the jail," he said quietly. "You haven't been there—yet."

A sudden silence closed down, through which Cortaro's lazy laugh flowed easily. He doffed his huge sombrero in a sweeping bow. "Touché," he said, and chuckled.

"Are you planning to linger in this vicinity?" Stuart asked.

Cortaro shrugged.

"Quien sabe, señor? One hardly knows in advance the will of fate. I 'ave the invitation from the Señor Broughton to visit at hees hacienda for a time. How long, you ask? Ah, who can tell?"

"Better watch your step, then. We ain't partial to gun fights in the Cibecue." The sheriff's agate eyes met calmly the other's hawk-like gaze. "If it comes to me that you've been participatin' in another smoke-and-lead affair in this county, I shall make it my business to see that you depart."

The fingers of Cortaro's right hand drummed his gun belt gently. "On the feet, eh?"

"On your feet or on a shutter—one."

"Ees that a threat?"

"That's a promise," Stuart's tone held no compromise.

Cortaro studied him wonderingly, his lower lip caught between even white teeth. Slowly he tapped his gun-butt to give emphasis to his words:

"You are one brave hombre, Tinbadge. *Si*— brave, but foolish, too. Men who use such words to Cortaro have been known to die sudden."

Stuart's tranquil glance wavered not a fraction. "Talk," he said, "is cheap."

It almost seemed to the onlookers that the sheriff was bent on driving the gun fighter to action. The townsmen held their breath and their muscles cramped.

185

Perhaps the same thought occurred to Cortaro. Certainly he made no move to grasp the gun that swung from his belt. Neither did he appear intimidated by Stuart's attitude. He remained his smooth, suave, bland and cunning self.

Languidly reaching upward with his right hand, he fished from the pocket of his pale blue shirt a packet of tailor-made brown-paper Mexican cigarettes, extracted one and returned the rest to the pocket. Gracefully he struck a match on his thumbnail and held one end of the cigarette to its flame in the most approved Mexican manner.

"Well," he said whimsically, "I shall not shorten my visit to this vale of tears by the inhalation of the fumes from the sulphur."

"No," Stuart grinned coldly. "You'll have a lot of time to inhale sulphur fumes after you leave."

Cortaro's teeth flashed in an appreciative chuckle. "Again touché! You are a rare one, my Tinbadge, truly. I wish we might 'ave met sooner. You do me good." His bright glance searched the sheriff's face. "Ah, well—vaya con Dios," and, with another chuckle, he followed the Circle B puncher into the night outside.

From where he leaned against the wall, Stuart heard the creak of saddle leathers, the jingle of spur chains, and soon the thudding sound of trotting horses. Gradually the sounds diminished until they faded in the vast silence of the night. Slowly, then, he turned and strode from the resort.

• • •

At the Broughton Ranch Dorinda heard the rhythmic clump of Tyrone's boots as he swung up the path toward the open ranch house door. Down the lighted hall she moved and paused inside the entrance, barring his way.

Tyrone came to a stop and looked up, grinning. "Wal, if it ain't Miss Dorinda, herself, in person!" he exclaimed, his eyes hungrily devouring her beauty. "This *is* luck—I didn't know if you'd be home."

"You wanted to see Jabe?"

"No, Jabe can wait. Shucks, I wanted to see you, Dorinda. Who'd wanta talk with Jabe when you're around the house?" he chuckled in what he considered to be a most jovial manner. "Shall we set inside or out?"

"I'm sorry, but I don't feel very much like conversation just now," she said.

"Sho, now, that's a shame."

"Yes—I've got a dreadful headache. I was going to lie down a while and see if it would go away."

"Gosh! layin' down ain't no way tuh get rid of a headache, gal. What you want tuh do is tuh get your mind off it. Yuh can't do that layin' down. Set out here on the veranda with me for a spell an' I'll talk that dang headache right outa your system!"

"But, really—"

"Shucks, Dorinda, don't hand me any buts.

Look at that big moon a-creepin' up over yonder there. Why, the night was just made for settin' on verandas," Tyrone said with appropriate gestures. "I can diagnose your trouble without no effort. You're lonesome, that's what ails yuh. What you need is a fella like me to set out with in the moonlight. Yes, sir—that's what you need, gal."

But Dorinda had a mind of her own, and the will to use it. She knew what she wanted, and what she did not want. And she was certain she did not want the company of Vic Tyrone, moon or no moon.

"I'm sorry, Vic, but really, I don't feel in the mood for moonlight," she told him frankly. "Some other time, perhaps—"

"See here, gal, I'm a busy man," Tyrone became impatient at such protracted dallying. "I've rode way over here just a-purpose tuh talk with you. Some other time won't fill the bill. I've got too much tuh do tendin' tuh ranch matters to come galloping over here every other flick of an ol' cow's tail, jest 'cause you've got a headache an' don't feel up to entertainin' company.

"You come out here on the veranda with me an' I'll do the entertainin'. I've got a question I wanta pop, an' I ain't a mind to pop it standin' here in the doorway like some mutton-headed catalogue peddler."

"You—you mean you want to ask me something personal?" asked Dorinda, surprised.

"Sure that's what I mean. An' let me tell yuh, the

question what I'm gonna ask you will send that headache of your'n skallyhikin' over into the next county!" He stood looking at her, grinning expectantly.

Dorinda stared at his perspiring countenance perplexedly. An inkling of his purpose began filtering into her consciousness. She looked at his flushed face and glowing little eyes more closely. Then, despite herself, she smiled—not at him, but at the idea she began to believe might lie behind his visit.

"Vic, you didn't ride over here with the object of courting me, did you?"

"Wal, an' what if I did?" He scowled, "Nothin' wrong in that, is there?"

"But, Vic—I'm engaged to Dan Stuart. I'm going to marry him."

He looked at her incredulously; chagrin, anger, resentment striving for mastery of his features. "But—but—Do yuh mean tuh say you'd take that wooden-faced block-head of a star-toter in preference to a man like me?"

She held silent, not knowing what to say.

He stared at her intently, while he grappled with this unforeseen development. Stark incredulity filled his gaze at first, then chagrin, embarrassment and anger stamped across his cheeks and his red-rimmed eyes grew ugly.

"So!" he snarled. "Yuh'd rather have that cheap, star-totin' grandstander, would yuh? Wal," he paused to slap his holstered gun for emphasis, "you can have him—or what's left of him when I git through!"

With a last malignant glare, he whirled and went striding savagely down the path.

20

When Dan Stuart took his departure from the Bucket of Blood Saloon, he headed thoughtfully toward his office. He strode slowly, mulling things over in his mind, attempting to pick out the salient points in this murder maze that confronted the Cibecue.

Exactly what grim knowledge or suspicion, he wondered, lay behind the troubled light he'd seen in Dorinda Broughton's eyes?

What dire secret had Caspar Druce and Big Cal Broughton shared that had made their deaths seem a necessity to the silent wielder of knives? Or did something else lay behind their tragic ends?

What man in this valley had the requisite nerve and skill to silence Campero in the midst of his revelations?

What man in this valley possessed the cold daring and determination necessary to enable him to return to the scenes of his crimes and recover the knives that had killed his victims?

What man had lain last night by the shadowy corrals across the street and pumped that shot at him as he had stood momentarily in the lighted office doorway? And had the shot been a warning, or intended death?

Would the pin marks on the shell he had found

correspond to the pin marks on a shell fired from Vic Tyrone's .30-.30?

Who was the killer of Cibecue, and would he, Dan Stuart, succeed in bringing the man to justice?

Would he be able to prevent the threatening range war that was spreading across the horizon of men's thoughts? Certainly, it seemed doubtful. It would, he was afraid, be well-nigh impossible should the unknown killer down another cowman.

So it all resolved to this: To prevent the range war, he must catch and punish the unknown wielder of the knife!

As Stuart strode slowly toward his office, glancing up, he saw the great lop-sided moon mounting the eastern heavens, mounting slowly, lazily, tranquilly, and he wished he might be riding with Dorinda instead of being cooped up here in Cibecue with a murder mystery on his hands.

His tired features twisted bitterly as he recalled his parting with the girl. When questioning her about the sheepman's camp, she had suggested that he had better leave. That had been hard enough to bear. But that had not been as bad a moment as, when after knocking her brother into the dust and ordering him back to town he had looked up to find her at the kitchen window.

Her subsequent actions, her odd stare and the lift of her chin when she had turned away, had spelled the doom of all his hopes. Their romance was ended; it was dead as last year's ashes. He had no need to hear her say so; he could see it for himself.

Whether it was his questioning, implying a possible doubt he did not feel; or whether it was his act in knocking down her brother that had turned the tide against him, he did not know. All he knew was that her love for him was gone—a thing of the past, a thing to be forgotten.

But he could not forget it, he told himself; it was a thing he could not bury. He would solve the riddle of these Cibecue murders, pull his picket pin and drift to fresher ranges. Any place would do, so that it lay far from here; any place where changing faces and a different life might tend to drive his thoughts from dwelling on the might-have-been.

In such a frame of mind the sheriff reached his office. Inside, the lamp still burned. But Nip Wingate and the car were gone. Stuart glanced around. The deputy had left no note telling of his destination.

Stuart closed the door with a weary shrug, drew the shades at the two windows and flung himself on one of the bunks to get what rest he might. No telling what the dawn might bring and he badly needed sleep.

As a result of his talk with Dorinda, Vic Tyrone was in an evil temper as he strode savagely down the path leading to the pole corrals that spanned the little creek. Turn him down, would she? Give him the horse laugh, eh?

An open anger burned sullenly in his cheeks and his red-rimmed eyes were ugly as he stamped savagely toward the corrals. He'd show the little huzzy! The danged little fool! He'd soon show her that it paid to be careful and pick the right man! By—! he'd make that wooden-faced star-toter hard to find!

Taking his rope from his saddle he pulled open the corral gate and went striding in among the horses. In a few moments he came striding out again, leading his captured horse. He was saddling the blue gelding when he caught the sound of approaching horsemen turning into the yard.

Pausing, he looked up and beheld two shadowy riders swinging down the aspen-bordered lane. Muttering to himself, he went on with his saddling, paying the newly come men no attention.

As they drew up nearby, away from the shadows beneath the trees, Tyrone saw from the corners of his eyes that the men were Blain and Glyman.

"What the heck!" said Glyman, surprised at sight of the Flying Star boss saddling up. "Meetin' all over?"

"To heck with the meetin'!"

"Cripes!" Glyman shoved back his hat and stared. "Somebody step on yore pet corn?"

"Mind your own business for a spell!" Tyrone ripped savagely.

"Jabe here?" asked Blain soothingly.

"I ain't seen him."

Blain and Glyman swung from their saddles, commenced stripping the gear from their horses. "Reckon we might as well wait," Blain said. They finished their chore and turned their mounts into the nearest corral. "Better stick around awhile, Vic."

Tyrone hesitated, then with a shrug, tethered his horse to the split pole fence and followed the others into the house. In the long main room, he flung himself into a chair and stared at his dusty boots absorbedly. Blain picked up a magazine and began thumbing its dog-eared pages. Glyman twiddled his thumbs, from time to time glancing covertly at the muscular owner of the Flying Star.

After a time Vic Tyrone got up from his chair and strode from the room. Blain and Glyman exchanged glances after he had gone. Blain winked. Glyman scowled.

"Somethin' sure set him on the prod, an' no mistake!" he muttered. "He acts madder'n a wet hen."

"He'll get over it," Blain grunted and returned his attention to his magazine.

Outside the house, Tyrone returned to the corrals, seated himself on the ground with his back against the poles of the nearest enclosure. His mind was at work on ways and means, apparently, for the sullen scowl still rode his cheeks.

Presently he heard again the thudding pound that proclaimed the approach of a horseman, but he did not move. He watched the blurred outline of a rider swinging down the lane between the rows of trembling aspens. It was Obe Shelty, he saw, and his lips curled in a derisive grin. Shelty, the loud-mouthed Marshal of Cibecue, an insignificant worm.

Before the marshal had finished stripping the gear from his lathered mount, Tyrone beheld two more horsemen riding toward him through the trees. One was a Circle B puncher, the other was a man he did not know—a stranger.

As they swung from their saddles close to Shelty, whom they ignored, Tyrone, concealed in the shadows, saw that the stranger was dressed like a Mexican. He wore a huge bell-crowned sombrero, a dark bolero over a pale shirt, chaps that glittered with silver, and a brass-studded gun belt whose Colt-filled holster swung at his groin.

"Cortaro!" he thought, and watched the man closely.

The gun fighter and his Circle B guide stripped the saddles and bridles from their mounts and turned them into the enclosure with Shelty's, Glyman's, Blain's and his own.

"Sure glad tuh have you with us, Mister Cortaro," Shelty piped up, in his reedy, bullfrog voice. "Them cussed sheepmen will clear outa the Cibecue on the run when they learn that you're here. Inside of two days, I'll bet there won't be a blattin' ba-ba left!"

Cortaro laughed softly.

Tyrone rose from his place in the shadows and strode forward into the moonlight, the soft jingle of his dragging spurs announcing his approach to the others who turned to watch him.

"Howdy Vic," the marshal said, with great show of cordiality. "Glad tuh see yuh. Vic, this is Mister Cortaro. Mister Cortaro, meet Vic Tyrone, one of our solid citizens, an' owner of the Flyin' Star."

The two men appraised each other carefully, then shook hands, apparently satisfied with what they saw.

"A leetle warmish, no?" said Cortaro.

"Yeah," Vic answered, "but it'll be a heap cooler 'fore mornin'."

"Is the Señor Broughton here? I have the so-kind invitation from him to visit hees hacienda."

"I understand Jabe's been in town all day," Tyrone answered. "But we're expectin' him back most any time now—" he paused. Borne on the close night air sweeping off the still warm desert, came the sound of a horse's galloping hoofs. "I reckon that'll be Jabe comin' now," he finished.

The men fell silent, scanning the shadowed approach beneath the trees.

In the corrals a horse stamped restlessly, as though knowing there would be further use of him before the coming of the dawn. Another rubbed its muzzle against the polished poles. The rank smell of their damp hides was in the air, and the odors of dust and leather and unwashed bodies.

But, try as he would and did, Stuart found that he could not control his roving, speculating thoughts long enough to woo the elusive god of sleep. There was no sense in his lying there, he told himself, unless he could sleep. So after fifteen or twenty minutes he swung his booted feet to the floor and stood up. Putting on his hat and pulling its brim down low across his haggard eyes, whose weariness he felt no need of concealing when alone, he left the office.

Above him, as he strode unhurriedly down the board walk that flanked the street, the stars shone like tiny lanterns against the purple bowl of Night. The dusty road between the buildings lay dappled and laced with strange designs in light and shadow, fantastic patterns cast by shadeless window and open door.

From somewhere among the moving shadows the rhythmic cadence of a horse's steadily-plopping hoofs drummed softly on the stillness.

Free! The thought came to Stuart with the force of an unexpected blow. *Free!*

Free to ride the range, that horseman. Free to ride wherever he might choose; free to do as he pleased and with no one to say him "Nay!" Free to ride where the fancy took him without thought of glinting star or oath-sworn duty to hold him to a single dangerous, distasteful course. Free to come and go.

Life, he thought morosely, was a hard and bitter thing to some. Life could do queer things to a man. There might be circumstances, he mused, where Life could make a man long for Death.

"A strange place, this world of ours," he muttered softly. "Sometimes gay, and sometimes sad—ofttimes bitter, an' mean, an' narrow. Shucks, a man ain't nothin' but a chip upon this checker-board of Life; a pawn moved onward willy-nilly to some strange, obscure, an' long-predestined end."

Looking up and finding himself across from the frame building lodging the Warwhoop Hotel, he bade adieu to his philosophic musings and, swinging from the walk, struck out across the street. Dust rose from the parched earth in billows at each step of his booted feet.

Reaching the opposite sidewalk, he paused to cuff his clothing, then strode through the open door into the dingy lobby of the town's only hostelry. The place was empty, as he saw at a glance. Wandering down a narrow hall he reached the kitchen where he found the proprietor immersed in a week-old paper.

Hearing his step the man looked up.

"Evenin', Gantley."

The Warwhoop's proprietor peered owlishly through his thick-lensed spectacles.

"Howdy," he said, curtly, and returned his attention to his paper.

"No one could accuse me of bein' over-popular in this man's town," Stuart thought grimly. But no emotion stamped, his cheeks. Aloud he said:

"Is Jabe Broughton putting up here, Gantley?"

The man rattled his paper irritably. "No," he grunted, and kept on reading.

"Can I ask another question?"

"Don't see no one tuh stop yuh."

"Well—has Jabe been stayin' here at all?"

"He's *been* stayin' here, but he ain't here now," snapped Gantley, and rattled his paper in a pointed hint.

But Stuart chose to ignore the man's manner. He was after information, and meant to get it. "When did Jabe check out?"

"My gosh, but you're persistent! Mr. Broughton left here about ten minutes ago."

"I don't suppose you happened to notice which direction he took?"

"He was headin' towards the livery, last I saw of him." Gantley eyed the sheriff coldly. "Anythin' else you'd like tuh know?"

"Well, not right now, thanks," Stuart said quietly.

When he reached the street, he diverged toward the livery. He found Smith rubbing down a lathered horse. "Whose nag is that?" asked Stuart.

"This here roan? Why, danged if I know what

the feller's name is. A stranger. Hit town last evenin' sometime, Sheriff."

Stuart described the dusty stranger he had seen several times last night.

"Yeah, that's him."

"Must have been in consid'rable of a hurry to wet his horse up that way," Stuart commented thoughtfully. "By the way, Smith: Has Jabe Broughton been around here?"

"Jabe? Why, sure. Jabe come here after his horse not more'n ten minutes ago."

"Didn't say where he was aiming to go, did he?"

"Wal, now, I don't know as he did," Smith answered slowly. "Leastways, I don't recollect it, if he did. Was you lookin' for him?"

"Not particularly. I kind of wanted him to stick around," Stuart said, "on account of the inquests we've got to have on Broughton, Druce, an' Campero. But I guess his presence won't really be necessary, though. The main thing I wanted him here for was to identify his Dad's body."

"His Dad's— Oh, yeah. I see," Smith muttered, and bent again to his work of rubbing down the stranger's lathered horse.

Stuart left him at it and strode up the street toward his office. The lamp was still burning he perceived. And the car was not in sight. Evidently Nip Wingate had not yet returned.

He strode inside and came to a pause beside his

desk. There on its surface, held down by one of Margate's missing knives, was a crudely penciled note:

"Sherrif:
    If yu aim tu know more about the killins whats goin on, get a warrant an search that ranch yu sold tu them damn sheep men. Hoskins office speshully."

There was no signature. But Stuart was in no doubt as to who had written it.

The thing was a red herring, he told himself, being dragged across the trail to distract his attention. A bluff. An empty gesture.

And yet, could he be sure it was? Supposing this was not a bluff—supposing that there was something at the S Bar 4 he ought to see?

"Dang it all," he muttered savagely, "I can't afford to pass it up!"

For several moments he stood there silently, re-scanning the scrawled message. Then he strode from the office, untethered his horse and swung to the saddle. He sent the buckskin out across the range at a jog-trot which, after a time, he increased to a fast lope.

Even in his own mind he was not sure whether he was riding toward Showlow because of this tip, or because his way led past the Circle B. But he was riding, and for the moment that was sufficient.

21

With the coming of night the desert sands cooled rapidly. A chill wind arose from off the waste lands. Cold and shrill it whistled through the cracks and crevices of Picture Rock. Cold and gusty, it shook and rattled the flapping canvas of the tent that had once belonged to Caspar Druce. Cold and mournful it sighed through the broad-leafed branches of the lone cottonwood, lending the gliding shadows beneath it life and grotesque form.

Rising from the brown-grass floor to the north, stark and bleak in the argent moonglow, Spotted Mountain reared its leprous slopes. Westward, slumbering in the monstrous hush that hung above it, lay the murky mass of gorges, rock-walled canyons, towering spires and precipitous pine-clad hollows called Blue House Mountain, frowning in somber disapproval upon the odoriferous flocks of sheep that lay bedded about its base.

Bruskell, the sheepman, stepping forth from the tent's interior, suddenly paused. From out of the night he had caught the muffled rataplan of a horse's hoofs. Steadily, inexorably, they drew ever nearer. Bruskell's hand reached down to the heavy gun that swung at his hip.

One of Bruskell's herdsmen came running up. There was a rifle in his hands; hoarse oaths came tumbling from his lips.

"Be still!" Bruskell growled, and a silence fell between them. The running horse was close; they could see him in the moonlight, his rider, hunched forward slightly, sitting motionless in the saddle.

The herdsman raised his rifle. Bruskell struck it down. "Stop it, yuh fool! That's Hoskins."

Hoskins brought his horse to a halt beside them and swung wearily from the saddle. He was a thin, sallow little man.

"What's the big idear?" Bruskell's voice issued gruffly around the stump of his black cigar. "I told you to keep away from this camp, Hoskins."

"I know it. But I've been in Cibecue tonight an' I heard somethin' I thought you ought to know."

"Yeah? Well, you're here now. Get it off your chest."

"Big Cal Broughton was killed last night—killed in town. Somebody stabbed him with a knife!"

In the moonlight Bruskell's face betrayed no feeling. For a long moment he remained motionless, a sinister, crag-like figure. No faintest flicker lighted his somber gaze.

"Well?" Hoskins' tone was a bit impatient. "Ain't you got nothing to say?"

"What did you want me to say?"

"Heck! Ain't that news significant?"

"How so?"

"Cripes! Do you think those cowmen are going to sit twiddling their thumbs?"

"I don't know," said Bruskell slowly. "They've got the best of it, so far. We've lost two—Druce an' Campero. A knife done their business, likewise."

Hoskins stepped back as though he had been struck. His eyes looked big and startled. "Druce? Campero?" He wet his lips. Consternation stamped his features. "No!" he muttered, and "No!"

"Yeah—Druce an' Campero. Look," Bruskell said gruffly, "look— If there's anybody got a kick comin' it's us."

"What are you going to do?" asked Hoskins, fidgeting with his tie.

"What would you do?"

"Gosh, I—I— I don't know, Bruskell. Maybe we'd better turn back. This Cibecue's a tough situation. The cowmen run this country—there's too many of 'em for us. This place ain't like New Mexico. They'll ruin us if we try to cross this valley."

"How else can we get to Showlow?"

Hoskins looked worried. "I don't like it," he muttered. "We'll never cross this valley. We—"

"Look," said Bruskell lazily; "How long you been with the pool, Hoskins?"

"Six years, pretty near, I guess," Hoskins' tone showed uncertainty, perplexity as to where the question was leading. But he was not kept long in doubt.

"You've seen some tough layouts, then. We cracked them, didn't we?"

"That don't signify," Hoskins muttered stubbornly. "We won't crack this one. It's different. There's never been any sheep in here before. They've never got as far as Blue House Mountain—"

"Nor as far as La Junta de los Rios," Bruskell cut in, "until we took 'em there. Look. I think your nerve is slippin'. I think you're gettin' a bad case of cold feet."

Hoskins made no denial. "What are you going to do?" he repeated.

"That depends."

"Heck! that ain't no answer. I'm askin' what you're going to do?"

Bruskell said, almost sleepily, "I'm goin' to wait for developments."

"Developments? Wait for another killing, you mean?"

Bruskell grinned.

"If I was you," his black eyes regarded Hoskins unblinkingly, "I'd keep away from Cibecue. It's a dang bad place to be seen after dark."

At the Circle B, the men before the corral relaxed as the oncoming rider drew clear of the murky shadows cast by the grove of aspens. Jabe Broughton had come at last.

He greeted them sourly as he dismounted, tethered his horse to the split pole fence. They moved toward the house in silence. When they entered, Blain rose to his feet.

"I'm sorry, Broughton, but I can't hang around any longer. I've got to be going."

"What's your rush?"

"No rush," Blain said. "I've been waiting here for two hours, now. I've sent two of my riders with fifty head of scrub cattle to the meetin' place near Spotted Mountain. I don't know if what we're plannin' tuh do is the square thing, in view of Stuart's stand on this sheep business, but anyways I'm wishin' yuh luck."

Tyrone grunted. Glyman winked as Blain left the house. "He's too dang scrupulous tuh suit my taste," he said. "What the heck's Stuart ever done fer us, I wanta know?"

Dorinda, after Vic Tyrone went striding savagely down the path toward the corrals, moved down the hallway thoughtfully. Going to her room, she sat down upon the bed, leaving the hall door ajar.

Tyrone's veiled threat left her filled with foreboding. She wished she had not told him of her engagement to Stuart. The sheriff could probably take care of himself, all right, but just the same she wished she had not spoken.

Vic Tyrone was a dangerous man. She had heard other people say so often enough. Too, she had heard the rumor that was being whispered to the effect that the boss of the Flying Star was on the make; that Vic Tyrone, in effect, was a rustler, a brand blotter, a thief.

As she sat there on the edge of the bed, she recalled the anger that had stained his cheeks when she had informed him she was engaged to the sheriff; she recalled the ugly light that had flared in his red-rimmed eyes. She recalled, too, his parting words: "You can have him—or what's left of him when I get through!"

A strange sense of uneasiness filled her as she sat there. Through the silence she heard the approach of horses, the creak of saddle leather and the muffled thudding of their hoofs.

After a time, she again heard hoofbeats and wondered what was taking place outside. Several minutes passed with dragging seconds. Once more she heard approaching horsemen. Curiosity mounted. She rose from the bed and, standing to one side of the window so as to remain unseen, she looked out upon the yard in the direction of the corrals. Several men were standing there, peering down the lane.

Another horseman was approaching. Her breathing quickened; it was Jabe.

What was he doing back from town? Were the inquests over? Or had Stuart given him permission to return?

She watched him swing from the saddle and

tether his mount to the split pole fence. The men were moving toward the house.

A few moments later she heard them enter, caught the sounds of muffled conversation, but could not make out the words. The front door closed and she heard the diminishing clump of receding boots.

Curiosity drove her to the door. She knew something of the ways of these self-sufficient cowmen, and knowing, she sensed that this was no ordinary friendly gathering. Something was afoot.

In her darkened room she had no great difficulty in persuading herself that she should know what was going on. She slipped out softly and tip-toed down the hall, to pause outside the open door of the long main room. The lamp that illumined the hall was bracketed to the wall above her head. She put it out.

After all, she told herself, she owned half the Circle B. She had a right to know what plans were being made. But she knew full well how carefully those plans would be concealed if she should enter the room; if the cowmen should guess that she was lurking in the hall behind the opened door.

She smiled faintly to herself and applied her eye to the crack that gaped between the hinges.

She could see Tyrone's sullen countenance, where he sat in a cowhide chair. She could see

Obe Shelty, the Cibecue marshal; Glyman; Jabe. Jabe was doing the talking:

"Tuh get their flocks tuh Showlow—to the S Bar 4, that is—the sheepmen has got tuh cross the Rim by that ol' trail northeast of Red Top Mountain. That's gonna carry 'em right past this ranch. By Gawd, fellas, I don't aim tuh have them stinkin' woollies tromp across my range! I make a motion we stampede the blattin' critters tonight!"

"That's talkin'!" Shorty Glyman approved. "I'm with yuh. Let's pull it off tonight."

"It's too late, now," Tyrone grunted, and swung his glowering glance on Jabe. "Where the heck you been?"

"Me, I been in town, that's where," Jabe swore viciously. "That dang stuck-up Stuart give me orders tuh stay in town till after the inquests. By cripes, he can whistle for me now!"

He glared about the room. "Do yuh know what? I jest found out Big Cal was murdered night 'fore last! Yes, by Gawd, an' that sneakin' Stuart was tryin' tuh cover it up!"

"Yeah—we heard," Glyman muttered. "Seems tuh me we ort tuh do somethin' about Stuart. He's sidin' with the sheepmen surer'n shootin'!"

"I guess they ain't no doubt about that," Jabe's eyes smouldered in his high-boned face. "First off, he sells his spread to a syndicate of wool-growers. Then when they show up, he comes down from Holbrook an' says there'll be no sheep-an'-cattle mix-up in the Cibecue. Then one of them blasted sheepmen knifes Big Cal, an' Stuart tries tuh cover it up."

Someone laughed, smoothly, easily; someone the girl couldn't see. "It would seem," said the owner of the laugh, "that El Señor Tinbadge has the valley bluffed."

Tyrone swore. Cords of muscle tightened along his jaw. His face grew dark with fury. He swung round in his chair toward the direction from which the laugh had come.

"You better turn that off, Cortaro. The laugh's gonna be on the other foot, pretty quick. That wooden-faced star-toter ain't puttin' anythin' more over on the cowmen of Cibecue Valley. He's about washed up. Even the townsmen are turnin' against him now. They don't like these knifings that are goin' on. If Stuart don't get the killer quick, he's finished in this country."

"So what?" came Cortaro's voice. "You are satisfied to leave it there?"

Tyrone's eyes shone a sudden icy blue between their red-rimmed lids. "What I'm satisfied to do," his voice purred softly, "ain't none of your danged never-mind, see?"

Dorinda's pulse had quickened at learning that the famed Cortaro was in the room. But now, at Tyrone's reckless words, she crouched breathless behind the door, waiting for the crash of guns.

But, strangely, the guns failed to roar. A long-

211

drawn moment passed in brittle silence. Then she heard again Cortaro's laugh. It flowed smooth and easy, no shade different than before. It took a brave man, she thought, to ignore the truculence that had been in Tyrone's ugly voice.

"You are entirely right, señor," came the gun fighter's liquid tones. "It ees none of my danged never-mind."

Dorinda saw the cords of muscle relax along Tyrone's set jaw. Slowly he turned, slumped back in his chair. But his expression remained sullen still. He sat with brooding glance locked on his boots. It was plain that the muscular rancher was in no happy frame of mind. She wondered if it was because of her, and decided that it was.

"It was not for pick the fight with El Señor Broughton's amigos that I 'ave been invited here, eh?" Cortaro said. "There is something you wish me to do, perhaps?"

Looking toward the gun fighter, Jabe nodded. "There's a jasper, name o' Bruskell, in the Tucumcari Pool. I reckon he's runnin' it, now. When we run our stampede through them sheep, I got a notion he's gonna go hawg wild. Now look. He's a bad actor, Mister, an' it may be that we'll give you the job o' takin' care of him, see?"

"It will be a pleasure, señor."

"I vote," squeaked Obe Shelty, in his high-pitched, bullfrog voice, "that we run that stampede tonight. Blain ain't real keen on it an' if we wait he might back out. I vote we go through with it tonight."

"That's so," Glyman seconded. "It'll look better for us if Blain has a hand in it. . . . Just in case some nosey jasper down tuh Phoenix happens tuh start an investigation, you understand."

Jabe, loosening the green scarf about his neck, noticed that Tyrone still seemed sullen. "What's got you on the prod, Vic? Yuh look mean as a prodded bull."

Tyrone gave him a sidelong stare.

"Did you know your sister aims tuh marry that dang wooden-faced star-packer?"

So, Dorinda thought, her engagement to Stuart *was* still bothering the boss of Flying Star!

"Who?" Jabe stared. "Stuart, you mean?"

"Yeah—Stuart."

"Like heck!" Jabe snarled. "She'll never marry him while I'm around the Circle B!" He stared hard at Tyrone, who had taken a bottle from the table and was worrying the cork from it with his teeth. "Where'd you git that dang fool notion?"

Tyrone got the cork out and, throwing back his head, took a good swig. He wiped his lips on the back of a hand. "She told me so herself—tonight, before you got back. I was gonna propose," he added.

Jabe stood there glowering. He ran his tongue across dry lips. Then—

"Look," he said. "How'd you like tuh have

Dorinda yoreself? She's right hard tuh manage sometimes. She's got a heck of a temper—headstrong like all us Broughtons. But with the right sorta handlin'— Wal, I reckon you could gentle her if yuh set yore mind to it."

Dorinda, crouching in the hall behind the door, felt hot color suffusing her face. Her hands clenched in indignation.

"Wal—do yuh want her?" Jabe's tone was impatient. "Speak up. We can't fool around here all night!"

Chagrin, resentment and finally something else, something Dorinda did not like, crossed Tyrone's mobile features. He took another drink from the bottle, a drink that emptied it.

"Yeah," he growled, "I'll take the uppity baggage—if only tuh put her in 'er place an' show that wooden-faced star-packer. By Gawd, I'll make 'er wish she'd kept her dang grins to herself! I'll make 'er wish she'd never been born!"

"That's all right with me," Jabe grunted. He stared at Tyrone even closer than before. "Now look—I got a proposition. We'll make a deal. If we come to terms, you get Dorinda."

22

"Oh," Tyrone said flatly. "You got a proposition—you wanta make a deal." He grinned sourly. "I mighta known a cold-jawed gent like you wasn't givin' somethin' away without a few ropes attached. Don't seem like you ever *do* give anythin' away, without yuh want a heap more in return."

"Heck, that's business, Vic! I got a head for it." Jabe produced a plug of tobacco and bit off a man-sized chew. "Wal, git yore mind made up. Like I mentioned before, we ain't got all night."

Tyrone's heavy face took on a scowl as he built himself a smoke. Licking the edge of the paper, he squinted steadily at Jabe as though weighing him, as though attempting to diagnose what lay hidden in his mind.

Tilting his head to one side, he said:

"Let's hear the proposition, kid—mebbe I don't want your sister so awful much."

"You hadn't ort tuh mind this deal much. It's all in your favor. Back me up in a finish fight ag'in' Stuart an' the sheepmen an' Dorinda's your'n."

Behind the open door, Dorinda clenched her fists until the nails bit into her palms. Her eyes were an icy blue as she stared at the gathering in the long main room.

Vic Tyrone was studying Jabe with unveiled curiosity. Glyman and Obe Shelty were grinning. Cortaro was outside her range of vision, so she could only guess what his expression must be.

The Flying Star boss put his twisted cigarette between his lips and struck a match. After blowing out a cloud of pale gray smoke, he drawled:

"It don't seem like you are makin' such a uncommon fine deal, Jabe. I'm against Stuart an' the sheepmen now. Don't hardly see how I could be against 'em any more than I already am. What's in your mind?"

"Look," said Jabe earnestly, "I need somebody I can depend on. These other fellas," indicating Glyman and Shelty with a jerk of his head, "might slide out on me if the goin' gits rough. But I know yore word is good. If you'll agree tuh side me in a finish fight the girl is yores."

Tyrone puffed on his cigarette. His dark, heavy-carved face with the scar on its forehead looked thoughtful. The ironic gleam, Dorinda saw, had left his eyes. They held now a steely glitter that cooled her angry blood.

He laughed abruptly. "All right, kid," he drawled. "It's a bargain. I figger we can smash that friend-sellin' Stuart to blazes, between us."

"Sure yuh can," Obe Shelty piped up. "An' with me an' Glyman an' Blain swingin' with yuh it'll be a lead-pipe cinch that Stuart won't last no longer than a June frost!"

216

"Yeah," Jabe grinned malevolently. "An' we've allus got Cortaro, here, as a hole card. Stuart can't buck us all an' win. This is gonna be his finish."

"Just why are you so dead set against the sheriff?" Tyrone questioned Jabe. "I don't recollect as he's ever done anythin' special to you that yuh should be so set on gettin' his scalp."

"He's done a-plenty," Jabe growled. "Why, heck, he beat me outa the sheriff's job, didn't he? Yeah, an' that ain't all I got ag'in' him—not by a jugful! I'll live tuh nail his hide to the fence, dang him, an' I won't take no rest till I do!"

Dorinda, seeing the smouldering flush on Jabe's high-boned face, recalled the scene in the ranch yard of this morning; the scene wherein Dan Stuart had knocked Jabe sprawling in the dust. She knew something of his vengeful nature, and realized that he would not be satisfied until that score had been evened up with interest. Jabe could nurse hate like an Indian.

She wondered where the sheriff was now. Thought of his efficiency, his calm tranquillity and self-assurance buoyed her in some measure; calmed the rising fear engendered by the steely glint she had seen in Tyrone's red-rimmed eyes.

As she thought of Stuart she realized that here was one man among ten hundred; he was not only as fearless a man as she had ever known—he was competent.

Still, as Jabe had said, he couldn't buck them all

and win. At least, it seemed to Dorinda highly improbable that he could. Certainly he stood scant chance of doing so unless he were warned of this conspiracy against him.

Bending, once more she applied an eye to the crack.

Tyrone had the appearance of a man who has recalled something important which had momentarily slipped his mind. He was getting to his feet and there was an odd expression on his heavy face as his little eyes swung to Jabe.

"Listen, kid," he grunted. "There's a story goin' round that your sister's handkerchief was found at Picture Rock last night beside Druce's body. How about it? Come clean now—was she there? If she was, Broughton, I'd admire mighty much to know what for."

For a fleeting second Jabe's mouth fell open. Then—

"How the heck did you learn that?" he blurted.

"Oh. She was there, then."

"When—where did you find that out?" Jabe snarled.

"Cripes, you ought to know by now such things as that travel some fast in this man's country. I reckon I knew about it dang near as quick as Stuart did."

Jabe Broughton's features were a study in conflicting emotions.

Dorinda Broughton's heart skipped a beat and

her pulses raced as she listened in growing wonder to Tyrone's words. So, *that* was where her handkerchief had gone! Her fears were realized. She had missed the bit of cambric when she had arrived in town last night. Had feared she might have dropped it in the sheepmen's camp. The last she remembered having it was when she had stood above the huddled form of Caspar Druce.

She saw now where Stuart's questions of the morning had been leading. He had known. Perhaps he had had the bit of cambric in his pocket at the time? Yet he had made no accusation! A glow of pride in his trust and faith suffused her body, but swiftly fled before a recollection. He had given her an opportunity to speak of her own free will—to explain the presence of her handkerchief in the Tucumcari camp. And she had not!

But she had told her father about going to Picture Rock, and had given him frankly her reasons for going. She had confided other things to him, also, when she had talked with him last night in town before going on to the Sheriff's Office. She had told him that Druce was dead.

For a moment, panic seized her. Could that fact in his possession have been responsible for his own untimely end? She shuddered at the thought.

Tyrone's rough voice brought her back to her surroundings with a jerk.

"Yeah," he growled, in evident response to something Jabe had asked him. "Like I said, I knew about the handkerchief business about as soon as Stuart did. An' what's more, I got a pretty good idear what Stuart did with it."

Dorinda saw that the others were watching the boss of Flying Star in expectant fascination.

"What?" Jabe whispered hoarsely.

Tyrone eyed the others with a grin. It was evident that he was enjoying himself.

"Cripes! If you don't hurry up an' speak—"

Tyrone chuckled. "No call to get excited, Jabe," he said. "The sheriff burnt it."

The others looked blank. Then someone swore.

"Burnt it!" Jabe snorted. "Of all the slat-sided, knot-headed fools—"

"What did you expect him tuh do with it?" Tyrone cut in. "Ain't he figgerin' to marry Dorinda?"

Jabe seemed astounded. It was plain that he was reluctant to believe anything good of his enemy. "Wal," he growled, at last, "it ain't gonna do him any good with me. I'm aimin' tuh lift his scalp jest the same."

"Naturally," Tyrone agreed. "Me, too. But lookit here, kid. You better get Dorinda in here an' see can we find out what the heck she was doin' at Picture Rock. I don't cotton to the idear of playin' second fiddle to no dang woolly-wrastler!"

Dorinda gasped, put a hand to her lips to choke off the sound. But the damage was done—the others had heard.

As she crouched there behind the door, for the moment too frightened to move or think, utter silence closed down on the room beyond. Then—

"What the heck!" growled Vic Tyrone, and started forward. With a muttered oath, Jabe swung into action in his wake, the others following.

At that sight Dorinda awoke to realization of her plight should the others catch her. She slammed the door and, whirling, sped down the ink-black hall. Her outstretched hands touched the closed front door, and the following instant her searching fingers found the knob and jerked the door wide.

She was outside and speeding toward the stable.

Luck was with her on this night. Halfway to the stable her probing eyes made out the forms of a pair of saddled horses hitched to the split pole fence. In an instant she was beside them. Tyrone and Jabe spewed from the ranch house door.

Her fingers seemed all thumbs as she tore at the knotted reins. But at last she had them free. She grabbed the nearest horse by the mane and with a bound was up in the saddle. Her spurless boots beat a hearty tattoo against the blue gelding's ribs and he lunged forward, encouraged by the sharp manner in which she brought the flat of her hand smashing down upon his rump.

In another moment they were plunging down the aspen-bordered lane among the shadows. Tyrone, Jabe and the rest were trying to head her off, running stiltedly toward the gate at the head

221

of the lane. Shouted threats and curses created bedlam in her ears.

"Hey!" Tyrone bawled at the top of his voice. "Stop, you little fool! That's my horse you got! Come back here, dang yuh!"

"Dorinda!" Jabe yelled viciously. "Pull up that nag or I'll give yuh a tannin' when I git yuh!"

But Dorinda paid no heed. She could see quite plainly that a number of unpleasant things were bound to happen if she stopped.

She whacked the gelding's ribs even harder with her heels and prayed for speed.

And then her luck seemed to run out.

Rounding a bend in the lane she saw that the gate was shut. Her heart almost stopped its frantic pounding.

Was this, then, to be the ignoble end of her gallant attempt to warn Dan Stuart? Was she to be balked at the very moment of her triumph by a paltry thing of wood and wire and nails?

She could have wept with chagrin, with rage.

But she did neither. Instead, she pointed the gelding's head straight at that low-hung gate, gave him a final desperate kick, and brought the rein-ends smashing down upon his flanks.

Down upon the gate they hurtled headlong. The startled cries and oaths of the running men were left behind as she lifted the gelding's head and put him at it.

She had no expectation that he would take the

jump—only a certainty of death. But even that, she told herself, was preferable to that which lay behind. She closed her eyes to pray, then opened them with a gasp.

The gelding had left the ground!

Straight and true he rose, lightly as a bird, and cleared the barrier safely.

23

"Cripes!" squeaked Obe Shelty's reedy voice. "She made it!"

Tyrone was staring incredulously after the madcap rider of the blue gelding. "Gawd!" he muttered, hoarsely. "I'd never of believed that nag could do it!"

Jabe Broughton came panting to a halt at the edge of the aspen grove, features taut and malevolent. Several times he made as though to lift one of the twin guns that swung at his hips, but each time appeared to change his mind.

"Be a shame tuh hit that geldin'," he scowled, and shook his fist at Dorinda's vanishing back. "Dang, bullheaded little fool!"

"The kind I like in my string," said Vic Tyrone, and chuckled to himself.

"I'll bring her back!" Jabe started toward the split pole fence where his horse was hitched. But a word from Tyrone stopped him.

"Let 'er go," growled the boss of Flying Star. "I'll see that she pays for her fun when I get hold of her. We got business tuh tend to now."

"That's jest it. If she gets tuh Cibecue and spills her news tuh Stuart—"

"Tut, tut. Time she gets to town, Jabe, we'll be close tuh Spotted Mountain an' dang near ready to start the stampede. Heck, Stuart'll never get to Picture Rock in time to save them blattin' sheep!"

"Yeah, but Stuart's prob'ly on—" Jabe began, and stopped.

Tyrone looked at him curiously. "On what?"

Jabe shook his head. "Nothin'," he said. "Ferget it."

"About the sheep," Cortaro ventured. "Do we ride tonight?"

"Yeah—c'mon," Jabe's angular rawboned figure slouched off toward the corrals. "We better get saddled up pronto an' on our way. We got no time tuh lose, tuh my way o' thinkin'—there's jest a chance that Stuart might make it. How many head would yuh say the boys are holdin' at Spotted Mountain, Vic?"

"How many you got out there?"

"Hundred an' fifty."

"I sent three of my boys out this afternoon with another hundred fifty," Tyrone said, rubbing his heavy jaw. "Blain claims he's about shoved in fifty, an' with Glyman's that averages roughly five hundred head. I reckon that ought to be enough to turn the trick, eh?"

"Sure ought to," Jabe grunted. "Anyways, we'll dang soon find out!"

As Dan Stuart rode easily through the moonlit night, he was thinking deeply, piecing together bit by bit the various strands that went to make up the rope of mystery that hung above the Cibecue.

In his own mind, now, he was satisfied that the unknown knifer must be one of four people. But strive though he did, he was at a loss to ascribe a sufficiently impelling motive to any one of the four.

To be sure, there were clues pointing toward each one of them; but nothing definite, nothing into which he could get his teeth. Even though the brass shell in his pocket should match a brass shell fired from Tyrone's .30-.30, nothing conclusive would be proved. It would merely signify that Tyrone was the unknown sniper who had taken a shot at him from the shadows of the corrals across from his office. But that did not prove that Vic Tyrone was the desperate knifer who, last night, had sent three men to their deaths.

Tyrone might have other reasons for wishing him out of the way. In fact, Stuart thought it quite probable that he had. The Flying Star owner was suspected of rustling. Knowing that he was so-suspected, Tyrone might have decided that Stuart was about to make an investigation. If Vic *was* a rustler—well, he'd be a fool to wait until the sheriff had proved it!

Of the other three men he suspected of being the possible killer, Stuart had even less to go on. Bruskell, to be sure, seemed a hard customer. Obviously the man was temperamentally suited to play the role of assassin without a qualm—if it suited his ends. But did it?

Dan Stuart did not know. He had found it impossible to penetrate the mask presented by Bruskell's inscrutable countenance. The man was hard enough and plainly clever enough to have been the author of these crimes. But the sheriff could perceive no possible motive compelling enough to have driven the man to murder. It hardly seemed probable, he thought, that Bruskell had murdered his uncle merely to gain his property and position as head of the Pool. And then there was the complication of Big Cal Broughton's killing.

Assuming that Bruskell *had* killed Druce, what possible reason could he have had for murdering Broughton, a man who was in town at the time of Druce's death? The theory that he had killed him because Broughton was head of the Cibecue cattlemen would not hold water—not in Dan Stuart's estimation.

And as for Jabe Broughton—well, Jabe hated sheep and sheepmen bitterly; he didn't appear to give a damn who knew it! But it did not seem possible that he could hate them sufficiently to steal into the sheepmen's camp and knife Druce. If he had done so, why had he not likewise murdered Bruskell and the other owners? The mere death of Druce, important though the man had undoubtedly been, would not hold back the others from attempting to take their flocks across the valley. It would need more than the single death of Druce to do that. And surely Jabe was smart enough to have seen that much.

Even assuming that he had killed the head of the Tucumcari Pool, there was still no explanation for the death of Big Cal. At least Stuart could think of no explanation that would tie in with the killing of the sheepman, other than that the murders were committed by different men. And this the sheriff did not believe. He was certain in his own mind that the three killings were the work of a single man.

The fourth possibility, the dusty stranger who had arrived in town on the eve of the knifings, seemed even more remote. Of course, he knew nothing whatever about the man. The fellow might have the very best of motives, for all Stuart knew to the contrary. But until he knew more about the man, he felt that he could not regard him as a very likely candidate. Too, he was rather slight in build, and apparently middle-aged. It had taken a strong, virile arm to wield those knives as they had been wielded.

Perhaps he ought to look into the stranger's credentials. Perhaps he had better check up on the man's actions since reaching the Cibecue.

There was one other possibility. These murders might be the culmination of something that had happened in the past—perhaps years and years ago. Feuds dragged on for years in this country, as Dan Stuart had every reason to know. But his attempts at digging something out of the past had so far met with scant success.

As he rode on across the moonsplashed range, heading for Showlow via the Circle B, a presentiment of impending tragedy gradually laid its icy fingers across the sheriff's mind. He tried to shake it off. In vain.

It was nothing tangible—nothing that he could explain away.

The moonlight, so bright at first, appeared now dim and hazy as though a screen lay across the silvery surface. The night silence seemed too deep, unstirring, dreary. There were none of the usual night sounds to break the brooding hush. Even the thud of the buckskin's hoofs seemed strangely muffled.

He tried to tell himself that it was because he was so dog tired that he was imagining these things, but the argument did not make them seem any less real. There was something wrong—he could feel it in the air. Even the buckskin's ears seemed to have taken on a forlorn droop.

Long cobalt shadows leaned down from the distant mountains and spread across the range. Here and there the terrain was dotted with the ghostly, smoke-like forms of blue salt cedars. Occasionally the octopus-like arms of ocatilla rose snakily from the sandy earth.

There was, Stuart felt, something sinister, malignant, in the brooding, waiting stillness.

He rode with weary eyes alert, and his rifle in his hands.

Out of the somber, moonsplashed silence drifted the wail of a coyote; a long-drawn note of incomparable melancholy, a drop of sound in the vast silence of timeless space. Brooding, primitive, Arizona stretched out about Dan Stuart from horizon to far horizon, shutting him off from the world of life and laughter—shutting him off from all save his gloomy thoughts.

His way at times led among blue-green sagebrush, thigh-high on a man. At other times the buckskin's hoofs trod clumps of bunch grass, brown and dry. Over all splashed the pale, dim light of the argent moon.

It was a world of slumbrous silence through which the sheriff rode his horse.

In the far distance, a dark blot against the pale horizon, Red Top Mountain reared its crest. In the nearer distance, dead ahead, Big Mountain squatted in melancholy solitude.

Something, far back in Stuart's mind, was struggling for utterance. Something he had learned but lately, but had not properly understood. Something, it seemed to him, significant—something that might well have a bearing on these killings. For a time he struggled to bring it forward that he might clarify it with mental vision. But it would not be dragged forth from its shadowy corner. The more he strove, the more stubbornly obscure it became.

He wondered what Dorinda was doing. Would he see her if he stopped a moment at the Circle B? Or would she already have gone to bed by the time he got there?

There was not much use, he thought, in speculating about Dorinda. Their love was dead, finished, washed-up. He had seen it in the odd look she had given him this morning when she stood watching from the kitchen window as he knocked her brother down.

He frowned. That vague voice at the back of his mind was stirring again; was trying to speak, to call his attention to something he had overlooked or had passed by with an indifferent glance.

But, as before, it failed.

He strove to break the depression, the despondency that gripped his spirit, but could not. The somber mood, the sense of impending tragedy would not be flung aside. This murder business was getting on his nerves, he told himself, and knew it was the truth.

He was weary—dead tired and weary of the entire tangle. If only the valley cowmen had the sense to see that the sheep syndicate simply *had* to cross the Cibecue to reach their newly-purchased holdings close to Showlow—the former Stuart ranch! If only they could have the wisdom to let the sheepmen go, making sure only that they went and did not linger!

But such hopes were futile, and Stuart recognized the fact.

Sheep were sheep! The cowmen did not want them—neither here nor at the S Bar 4, which lay much too close for the cowmen's liking. And deep in his heart Stuart did not blame them.

Sheep were sheep!

Cattle would not, even if able, graze where sheep had passed until months after their passing. Usually they were not able, for sheep had a trick of eating the grass to its very roots.

And there was more to it than that, of course. When one sheepman grazed in peace, twenty others would flock to join him. Followers of the grass, they went wherever they dared. Grass, always grass—grass was the sheepman's god!

Stuart came from a long line of cattlemen. Hatred of sheep had been formed in his bones, hatred of sheepmen had been fed him with his mother's milk. He had been raised on the curse of sheepmen and their dirty flocks.

At a tender age he, like other cattlemen's sons, had been taught to believe that nothing was too low-down for a sheepman to commit in his everlasting lust for grass. The breed, he had been schooled, would cheerfully bribe, kill or murder—anything to get the coveted grass, grass, grass for their bleating flocks!

In his own case, it had been amply demonstrated by the Tucumcari Pool in the trickery by which they had gained possession of the S Bar 4.

But, despite all this, Stuart was still unswerved, unbending in his inflexible determination to prevent a sheep and cattle war in the Cibecue. He would prevent it if its prevention cost him his very life. The lives of too many others were at stake; lives for which he felt himself responsible, since it had been he who had sold the hated sheepmen land.

He recognized that he could never hope to prevent the threatening war if the Cibecue killer continued wielding his deadly knife. The man, whoever he was, must go!

Abruptly, to the sheriff's ears, came the drumming pound of a hard-running horse. Faint at first as though with distance came the thunder of pounding hoofs. Then swiftly it rose, as though the rider had clattered up some distant rise, and slowly dropped once more as though he were speeding down a descending slope.

The sheriff's pulses quickened to that muffled, beating tread. He scanned the country round about with thoughtful, narrowed eyes. He glanced upward into the purple dome of heaven and saw by the moon's position that it must be nearing eleven o'clock. No man, he knew, nor woman would drive a horse at that breakneck pace unless it were imperative.

Suddenly he made out the rider. Far away across the undulating surface of the range a thin, wavering line of dust streamed out and trailed away in the quickening breeze. Just ahead of the wavering smoke-like film sped a dark lot against the earth—a dot that was rapidly drawing nearer.

The beating hoofs, as the minutes passed, rose loud in volume, swelled like rumbling thunder on the rising wind, swept forward like the muffled roll of drums.

Eight hundred yards away the horseman dropped from sight, but the sound rolled ever on.

Then abruptly, out from a shallow arroyo, came the crazily-ridden horse, splashing sand hat-high under the stinging bits of rein and boot.

Stuart kneed his buckskin broadside to the coming rider, and with ready rifle waited, eyes slitted, cold and steady.

But suddenly they bulged as the horseman drew up in a sliding cloud of dust, and he found the white face of Dorinda peering into his own.

"Quick! For God's sake, hurry!" her voice was panting, filled with passion. "Swing that horse an' head for town! Blood stampede! Cowmen! Picture Rock!"

24

Perhaps now, for the first time since she had known him, Dorinda was glimpsing something of the vast difference in temperament which lay between herself and the Sheriff of Navajo County.

Her hard riding since fleeing the Circle B had driven most of the color from her cheeks. She had driven the roan for all she was worth in an effort to warn this man of the cowmen's plans in time to block them. Why did he sit there eying her so strangely when every wasted second was precious?

He sat his horse in the moonlight, yet shadows lay dark upon his face. He leaned forward and she beheld it plainly and was shocked at the change that had come over him since this morning when he had eaten breakfast at the ranch.

His maddening tranquillity still lay heavily upon him—but there was something else, something new and different about his features. His face was haggard, weary, bitter. The strain and fatigue of the past thirty-odd hours was taking its toll of him. His tight-pinched lips held a sardonic curve. Deep-etched lines ran upward from their corners to the wings of his nostrils. There were black circles under his bloodshot eyes.

"Seems like you're just a little worked up this

evenin', Dorinda. 'Pears like you ought to rest a bit," he drawled, in a strangely lifeless voice. "Ain't that Vic Tyrone's nag you're forkin'?"

"What of it? Don't you understand what I've been telling you? The cowmen under Jabe and Vic are going to run a stampede through the sheepmen's camp before dawn! If you want to avert this range war, you'd better swing that buckskin an' ride!"

"Don't seem like there's such a mighty call for hurry. You ought to walk your roan up an' down a bit. This wind's gettin' cold—he won't be worth much if he cools too quick."

"Are you going to ride to Picture Rock, or not?" she demanded curtly.

"I reckon I'll ride when I get ready. You better walk that horse, Dorinda—"

"Oh, drat this horse!" she lashed back at him. "Sometimes, Dan Stuart, I almost hate you!"

"Well, now, I reckon that ain't so odd. I guess you got cause to feel a little proddy after the way I knocked your brother down this morning. I reckon I understand how things are between us. I—I won't be botherin' you any more, ma'am."

"What on earth are you talking about?"

"Why, about you an' me, ma'am. A—About our engagement. I—"

"But, Dan! Don't you realize that every second we sit here may be precious? The cowmen are holding a herd of mixed cattle at Spotted

Mountain. As soon as Vic and Jabe can get there they'll start the stampede!"

"Yeah, I understand. I been expectin' them to do somethin' like that. I figure I can get there in time—"

"I'm going with you," she cut in.

"I don't reckon you'd better do that, Dorinda. Picture Rock ain't gonna be no good place for a woman when I get there. I'm a heap obliged to you for bringin' me word—mighty decent of you under the circumstances."

"Save your thanks. I'm going with you," there was determination in her tone.

Stuart, reognizing that her mind was made up, offered no further argument. "I would sort of like to explain why I struck Jabe—"

"You don't have to. I heard the whole thing," she said. "I understand some things now that I couldn't figure out before."

"Yes, I—I saw you at the kitchen window. I— Well, I reckon that's all, Dorinda. I guess I understand how you feel about everything. About my questionin' you this mornin' about going to Picture Rock last night an'—"

"Whatever are you talking about, Dan Stuart?"

"Why, about us not being engaged any more," he answered dully, his tired eyes brooding on his saddle horn.

"Who said we weren't engaged any more?" she looked at him wildly.

"Why, I sort of figured when I saw you lookin' at me so odd this morning—"

"If I looked at you oddly, Dan, it was because I was realizing what a fool I had been in not seeing sooner why you were so determined to prevent trouble between the sheep and cattle interests."

"You—you mean you know?"

"I think I do, Dan. Somehow you were tricked into selling your ranch to the sheepmen. I couldn't understand your actions until I heard Jabe accuse you of selling out to them this morning. Then it came over me all of a sudden that they had tricked you into it somehow.

"I understand now. You feel yourself responsible for the sheepmen being here. You feel that if a bloody range war starts, it will start because you have been tricked into selling land to Druce and his partners. You feel that any loss of life resulting from such a war will be your fault. Isn't that so?"

He sat looking at her wonderingly, almost eagerly.

"An'—an' you ain't aimin' to break our engagement?"

"Of course not, Dan—"

His horse jumped forward beneath his spurs and the next moment she was in his arms, and the fragrance of her hair was mounting to his nostrils. As he felt her cool, moist lips upon his own, love flowed through him like a rare wine. "Oh, Dan—"

her voice held a liquid softness as, leaning from their saddles, their upper bodies made a single shadow on the ground.

"I reckon we better be goin' now," he said, after a little while.

"Yes," she straightened in her saddle, "I suppose so." Somehow the sheepmen's troubles did not seem so urgent now. "I—I wish you didn't have to go on with this, Dan. So many people have turned against you. The cowmen and the townsmen—I don't think even the sheepmen fully trust you. I don't see how they could dare, after the way they tricked you into selling them land."

"I know. I wish I didn't have to go on with this, too. But I have, Dorinda. I can't get away from it. We can't help being what we are, and bein' so we have to do the things we have to do. It's destiny— there's no gettin' away from it. If I left this thing to work itself out, I could never hold my head up again. I couldn't look a man in the eye—my conscience wouldn't let me."

He looked at her hungrily. "I—I'd like to oblige you about this, Dorinda, but it jest ain't in the cards."

"I hate fatalism!"

"Sure, I know you do," he said, and turned his eyes across the range. "I don't know as I'm a fatalist, exactly. It's only that I'm built a certain way—I have to do the things that to me seem right. I—I couldn't run away from this, Dorinda. I got the cowmen into it by sellin' my spread to sheepmen. I got to keep the cowmen from gettin' themselves into trouble. There can't be no side-steppin' now. We got to face this thing."

"Oh, Dan— Can't we go away?"

"I reckon not, honey. You wouldn't want a man that ran from trouble—trouble that he started his own self—" He paused abruptly, staring out across the rolling, moonlit range.

Dorinda, looking at him, saw that his cheeks were taut, that cords of muscle stood out rope-like along his jaw. She turned to follow with her eyes the direction in which he appeared to be staring.

Far out on the valley floor a mounting dust cloud trailed a group of speeding dots. At the sight she stiffened, and a cry that was like a groan came from her parted lips:

"The cowmen!"

"Yeah," Stuart picked up the reins. "They're headin' for Spotted Mountain. We still got a chance to beat 'em to Picture Rock. C'mon, gal— roll your steel!"

As they swept into motion, dust and pebbles spurted up from the thudding hoofs of their hard-running broncs. Inside of twenty yards they were pounding forward at a dead run.

Across the undulating plain they moved like windblown shadows. Each long powerful lift of their horses' legs was fraught with desperation.

The wind rushed against them, struck their faces like an unseen wall. It shrieked an anthem in their ears, an anthem punctuated by the rhythmic pound of the horses' flying hoofs.

From the tops of frequent rises they caught fleeting glimpses of the vast country spread out about them. It stretched before them mile on mile in the argent light of the sliding moon. A mighty world of moonlit silence, space, and desolation; majestic in its brooding, solemn beauty.

Time meant everything now. The safety, indeed, the whole future of the Cibecue might well depend on their reaching the camp at Picture Rock with time to spare before the stampeding cattle hove in sight. The sheepmen must be warned. If the cowmen's frenzied cattle were turned upon the sleeping sheep of the Tucumcari Pool, nothing under God's heaven could save this range from war!

Stuart rode with his slitted eyes fixed straight ahead toward the towering spires of Blue House Mountain. He did not use his spurs, now, nor the quirt of braided leather that hung from his saddle horn. He rode hunched forward in his saddle.

Down a narrow, treacherous trail they thundered—down into an arroyo. Along its bottom they raced for fifteen minutes, then climbed a cut bank and flew on across the rolling desert floor. Before them Blue House Mountain loomed larger, nearer, clear-cut against the starlit sky.

No longer could they discern the dust cloud which had marked the cowmen's progress.

"Streakin' along a gully someplace," Stuart shouted. Dorinda shook her head to show she heard.

"They ain't got so far to go as we have," Stuart added, "but it'll take 'em a spell to get their herd in motion. We'll beat 'em yet to Picture Rock!"

25

Jabe Broughton, Vic Tyrone, Glyman and Cortaro and Obe Shelty came spurring into the cow camp near the base of Spotted Mountain just three hours short of dawn. Swiftly they flung themselves from their blowing horses, stripped the gear from their backs and turned them loose. The wrangler brought up fresh mounts from the cavvy and the cowmen threw their kaks upon them and hurriedly cinched them down.

Tyrone sent up a bellow for his foreman and when the man slouched up:

"Have yuh got them slaughtered beeves ready?"

"Sure thing, boss. We got 'em cached down the draw a piece where the wind won't carry the smell to the herd. Yuh want we should get 'em now?"

"Pronto!" Tyrone snapped, and, flinging out swift orders, the foreman grabbed a bronc and went spurring off.

Blurred shapes of horsemen rode slow monotonous circles round the sleeping herd. The waiting cowmen, standing round the chuck wagon fire, caught occasional snatches of chanted song from the lips of the men on circle:

"Down in the horse corral
Standin' alone
Is this ol' caballo,
A strawberry roan,
His legs is all spaven,
He's got pigeon toes,
Little pig eyes
An' a big Roman nose."

The Flying Star foreman, with a rope in each hand, came up. The end of each rope was made fast to a fresh hide. Two other men followed him, each with a rope about a dragging, freshly-skun carcass.

"Think two steers'll be enough?" asked Jabe.

"Hell, yes! Two carcasses an' two hides ought to be enough tuh stampede any man's herd, with the wind blowin' right," Tyrone answered. He turned to the foreman: "Call in the boys that's ridin' circle."

When the riders who had been singing to the herd came jogging in to the fire, Vic Tyrone looked them over and at Jabe's nod apportioned two to either flank; they waited five minutes to be sure the Hankers were in position, then Vic, Jabe, Shelty, Glyman, Cortaro and several extra punchers began firing their guns into the air and howling like Comanches. Two or three rode toward the herd waving slickers.

Came a rumble of hoofs like sullen thunder amid

the criss-cross lightning of belching guns. Like a single steer the herd reared up on its feet, whiffing, snorting, bawling. As the blood smell from the fresh hides and carcasses came down the wind, guttural grunts, bellows, blats and high staccato screams filled the darkness of early morning.

Then came the shrill, demoniac blood cry that sent the herd pounding into a heavy run, horns down and eyes rolling. The stampede was off!

Across a dry wash they thundered, and above the pounding hoofs, the rattle of clacking horns, the bawlings and bellowings, came the crash of exploding six-shooters and the high yip-yip-yipping of the pursuing cowmen.

"Hump, you cow critters! Git along, git along!"

The flanking horsemen kept the rolling herd pointed head-on toward Picture Rock. The riders dragging the carcasses and fresh hides tossed the ropes that dragged them about the horns of the hindmost steers to keep the blood-smell fresh in their nostrils.

Topping a low ridge looking down upon the camp at Picture Rock, Tyrone and Jabe signalled the riders to drop back.

"Git on, yuh dang dogies! Roll on, roll on!"

Down the ridge with clacking horns, down upon the sheep camp half a mile away, rolled the bawling horde of stampeding cattle.

"That'll fix them stinkin' sheepmen!" said Vic Tyrone, with a saturnine chuckle.

"By Jésu, yes!" agreed Cortaro, watching. "Sangre de Dios! by dawn those sheeps won't be nothing but the bad memory round here!"

The lathered horses of Stuart and Dorinda were beginning to falter in their stride as they drew in sight of Picture Rock. A rifle shot beyond rose the towering rock escarpments of Blue House Mountain. The riders could see a low ridge that rose from the plain to the northeast—toward Spotted Mountain where the cowmen held their restless herd.

Stuart glanced up at the waning moon. Dawn, he thought, was still nearly three hours off.

The air was pungent with the mingled scents of windswept pine and juniper. But slowly another scent became apparent, a different smell that grew ranker and stronger with each hard-won stride of the laboring broncs—the acrid stench of hated sheep!

Stuart shook the weary droop from his shoulders. "I'll do the talkin'," he flung back at Dorinda, riding half a length behind. "Bruskell ain't going to like this news we're bringin' him. The less you say the better for all concerned."

The girl jerked her head to show she understood.

Bruskell's camp lay close ahead now. They could see it plainly, with the bedded flocks beyond. Bruskell's tent lay dead ahead, sheltered by rocks and a lone cottonwood tree. Further on were more trees.

When they were still over a hundred yards away the dogs set up a fierce barking that roused the camp.

Bruskell stepped from the tent, a rifle in his hands. Another man appeared, took up a position a little to one side, a hand on a holstered weapon. Men appeared running toward them from the wagons.

Stuart and the girl swung from their blowing horses beside the tent. The sheriff saw that the man with Bruskell was Hoskins, secretary of the Pool. He grinned faintly.

"Evenin' Hoskins. Howdy Bruskell."

"Look," said Bruskell gruffly, the everlasting black cigar-butt gripped in his strong white teeth. "What do you want here, Stuart?"

"I'm here to warn you, Bruskell. Miss Broughton rode to tell me the cowmen are planning to run a stampede through your flocks before dawn. You've got no time to lose if you want to save your sheep."

"I don't quite get this, Stuart. Look—you're a cowman, or was till we foxed yuh into sellin' us the S Bar 4. How come you're goin' outa your way to do the Pool a favor? Hah? It looks dang queer to me—uncommon odd, I'd call it."

"Call it whatever you want," said Stuart coldly. "I'm tryin' to avert trouble between sheep an' cattle in the Cibecue. That's the only reason I'm warnin' you. Don't think I'm doin' it out of love."

"I think you've got some slick scheme up your sleeve, Sheriff," said Bruskell, heavily, suspiciously. "You're tellin' me this in the hope I'll turn the sheep—"

The moon lay bright upon Stuart's face. Dorinda, watching him as he stood there confronting the sheepmen, saw a rare flush of anger come into his haggard cheeks. His voice was thick:

"Quit playin' the fool, Bruskell! Either do somethin' to save these sheep, an' do it quick or, by Gawd, I'll do it for you!"

Bruskell betrayed no feeling. He stood motionless, a sinister, crag-like figure, his black eyes searching the sheriff's face with unblinking intensity. Still without moving, he raised his gruff voice:

"Hey, you fellas!" he bellowed at the men who were running toward them from the wagons. "There's a blood stampede on the way! Get out that wire an' string it fast!"

The running men checked their stride, turned and raced back toward the wagons, cursing.

"So you think I've been playin' the fool, do yuh?" Bruskell's cold black eyes bored Stuart's.

Stuart's agate eyes met Bruskell's unwaveringly. "You have. No bunch of sheepmen, however tough, can hope to beat the cowmen of Cibecue Valley in their own stamping grounds. You're

248

attempting the impossible, hombre, an' the sooner you realize it the better it's goin' to be for all concerned. If you'd had a lick of sense you'd have turned your sheep back before this. You'll never cross the Tonto Rim with these flocks."

"Look," grunted Bruskell heavily, "I've got a ranch near Showlow. Do yuh think I want to leave it settin' there idle?"

"I've offered to buy that ranch back," Stuart answered low-voiced. "The offer is still good. Call it quits now, return the deed to my office in Cibecue, and I'll write you out a check coverin' every cent Druce paid."

"Ah." A faint smile edged Bruskell's red-stubbled lips, but the black eyes above it were opaque and hard. "So this warnin' is the bunk—yuh're tryin' to force me out."

Stuart's lean square jaw looked grim. "Listen, Mister. If I saw any way to force you out I'd take it. As it happens, though, this warnin' is straight goods. Listen—"

Drifting on the cold wind that swept the moon-lit range came a faint bawling of cattle, a low, rumbling thunder that created a tremor of the ground. Bruskell's face creased tight about the cigar stump in his mouth. Still he stood there motionless.

They could hear the coming cattle plainly now. The sound was like the rumbling growl of distant thunder sweeping in along the ground.

Camp-movers, herders, wagon bosses and cooks scurried back and forth among the trees stringing their deadly barbed wire entanglements. They moved with frantic haste, for they, too, could hear the ominous sound and the muffled *pop-pop-pop*-ing that was the reports of guns.

Stuart's haggard features grew pale as he watched their preparations, for he knew what barbed-wire would do to running cattle. It would saw those running steers in two if they ever struck it at the pace those rumbling hoofs denoted. It would rip their chests out like a surgeon's knife. It would turn that thundering herd to buzzard bait. But it would not stop the cowmen. Nothing, Stuart thought, would stop them until the last dirty sheep had left the Cibecue.

Now, looking out toward the distant ridge, the group about the tent could see the oncoming flood of tossing horns and rolling beef. Like a mill race it came rumbling down the slope.

Bruskell gripped his rifle tightly, swore, and broke into a run to place himself behind that strung barbed-wire; dragging out his pistol, Hoskins followed.

Stuart turned to Dorinda, who, white-faced, was watching the oncoming sea of cattle.

"Come on," he said wearily. "I reckon we've done all that we can do. We might as well shag along back toward town."

26

To the watching group of cowmen, sitting their horses on the ridge, the sudden checking of the bawling herd seemed miraculous. Hardly had they hit the line of trees than something appeared to wedge them there, the cattle behind came pressing in, goring the ones in front, climbing up atop their backs—it was like a log jam in a river, and just as costly.

Jets of flame licked out from behind the trees where the moonlight glinted on the polished tubes of steel that were rifles in the sheepmen's hands. But it seemed impossible that the rifle-thrown lead alone could have stopped that wild stampede, or caused that piteous, hopeless bawling that rent the air.

The stampede was finished, and without ever touching the sheepmen's flocks; checked and slaughtered at that shadowy line of trees.

Jabe swore wild bellowing, ranting curses; fired his pistols futilely at the distant camp. His anger was a vile and horrible thing. He cursed the sheepmen. "They been warned, dang their hides!" He cursed Dorinda, whom he rightly suspected had warned Dan Stuart. He cursed the sheriff, whom he believed had warned the camp at Picture Rock. He cursed his companions and his Maker!

"Choke off the blat, yuh fool!" snarled Vic Tyrone. "I'm jest as mad as you are, but I ain't findin' it necessary to run off at the mouth. Stow it, dang yuh! I wanta think."

Jabe turned on him with lifted guns.

"More o' yore dang foolishness," Tyrone sneered. "Them guns is empty, yuh slat-sided nitwit! Yuh jest finished emptyin' 'em pluggin' holes through the air! Get a holt on yourself!"

Still cursing, Jabe fumbled at his belts, began stuffing fresh cartridges into the hot chambers of his guns. "Them sheepmen was warned!" he shouted. "I tell yuh, some—warned 'em!"

"'Course they was warned—any dang fool could see that with half an eye!" Tyrone flung back. "Trouble is, knowin' they been warned now ain't doin' us any good. There's at least ten thousand dollars gone tuh blazes on a pinto in that fool stampede! An' what've we got to show fer it? Hey? Not one single lousy dead sheep! Ten thousand dollars shot plumb tuh hell by a mess of rusty barbwire!"

"Nobody but a stinkin' sheepman would use barbed wire on a herd o' cattle!" Jabe slobbered in his rage. "By—! hangin's too good fer 'em! They oughta be drug ten miles by their thumbs, boiled in lard, an' have splinters stuck in their eyeballs!"

"Stuart's the one we gotta get fer this," Tyrone said malignantly. "Dorinda might tell Stuart about our stampede, but she'd never tell no blasted sheep-grower! Dan Stuart's the one that did us this dirt!"

"An' by—, we'll git Dan Stuart!" Jabe snarled, showing his yellowed teeth. "Cortaro!" he rasped, "come over here!" and led the way aside, Tyrone following, out of earshot of the others.

"We're goin' tuh fix Stuart first, then we'll get Bruskell," Tyrone told the gun fighter, when they had drawn away from the other cowmen sufficiently to make sure their conversation would be private.

"Now here's the way I look at it," Tyrone went on softly, head thrust to one side. "Bruskell is this here Cibecue killer—there can't be no doubt about that. Only a stinkin' wool-grower would stoop to usin' a knife—'specially on a fella's back. Now—"

"But why should Bruskell wish to keel his uncle?" Cortaro asked.

"How'n heck do I know what a sheepman's reasons are. They don't reason. They're like their bleatin' woollies! Probably he wanted to control the syndicate an' get his uncle's share. Heck, sheepmen is the greediest humans on Gawd's earth, fella! Now then, here's where you come in. You're a professional gun slinger. What'll yuh charge to kill a man?"

The cold, bloodlessly handsome face of the gun fighter grinned. "Which man?"

Tyrone turned his red-rimmed eyes on Jabe.

Jabe said: "Stuart,—his soul!"

Cortaro turned a glance across his shoulder to where Obe Shelty sat his horse with Glyman and the waiting punchers.

"Cripes, don't worry about that wart!" Tyrone snorted. "He don't amount to no more in this country than a June frost!"

"He lives fer votes," Jabe put in with a sneer; "We give 'em to 'im."

Cortaro shrugged. "What will you pay, señors?"

"Name your price!"

Cortaro spread his palms. "The Señor Stuart ees a heap uncertain to monkey with," he said slowly. "I think five hundred dollars, Americano, would be a fair price for keel this man."

"Five hundred dollars!" shouted Jabe. "What the heck d'you take us fer? We just lost ten thousand dollars in this stampede!"

"*Si*—quite so," Cortaro laughed, smooth and easy. "Hombres that can lose ten thousands dollars in one fool stampede, can pay five hundred dollars to remove the cause of their loss, I should theenk, *no?*"

"Cripes!" snarled Vic Tyrone. "Is your name Jesse James?"

"No—Cortaro," said the gun fighter, and chuckled pleasantly. "Five hundred dollars is my price, señors, an' cheap at that. Eef the señors do not wish to pay so much, then let the señors keel this hombre themselves."

Tyrone looked at Jabe.

Jabe looked at Tyrone. Jabe said, "All right—
five hundred bucks, dang yuh. Let's hit fer town
an' get it over."

27

Stuart and Dorinda, heading toward town, rode for some distance in silence, rode until the faint sound of rifle fire drifted to their ears.

"Sheepmen," Stuart said gruffly. "Reckon they're gettin' in a few licks while the cattle pile up on their danged wire."

"Couldn't you have stopped it, Dan?" the girl asked, hesitantly, looking toward him, but unable to see his features because of the darkness which now, just before dawn, lay heaviest across the range. "Wasn't there anything you could have done?"

"Don't hardly see how there was, Dorinda. It was my duty to warn the sheepmen so's they'd have a chance to save their flocks from that stampede. They saved 'em," he added grimly, "in the only way they could. It was hell, I don't deny. But I warned the cowmen publicly not to start anything against Bruskell. They'll have to take their loss, I reckon. It ain't near as bad as it might've been—most of the cattle in that stampede was scrub stuff."

As they neared the town, they saw that in the east a faint line of gray was lightening the rim of the world. Dawn lay close at hand.

"Was you figuring to stay in town, or go on

home, Dorinda?" Stuart asked. "If you want to go home I'll take you in the machine, if Wingate's got back with it."

"I shall never go back to the Circle B while Jabe is there," she said with passion.

Stuart looked at her, wondering at the tremor in her voice. But it was still too dark for him to make out her expression. Her face was a gray blur against the range.

"Why, Dorinda—did something happen there last night?" a steely note had crept into Stuart's voice. "If any one of them—"

"Nothing happened," she said quickly—too quickly the sheriff thought. "I'll put up at the hotel."

"Well, perhaps that would be better. Stayin' alone at isolated ranch houses ain't apt to be a heap safe while this Cibecue Killer's rompin' round the country. With a little luck, I'll maybe get him today. Sooner or later he's bound to show his hand," his voice trailed off and lapsed into silence.

They entered Cibecue's dusty street. It was getting a little lighter now, but objects at any distance were still vague and formless. They turned down the street toward the hotel. As they passed the Sheriff's Office, Stuart noted that the machine was parked before the corrals across the street. Evidently Wingate was back.

"Dan," Dorinda reached out and laid her hand

upon his arm. "Dan, if you'll come to the hotel in an hour or two, I'll—I'll tell you about how my handkerchief came to be found at Picture Rock."

Before Dan Stuart could find his voice, she had flung from her horse and was running up the hotel steps. Stuart pushed back his hat, rubbed his forehead with a puzzled hand.

He turned his horse toward the livery.

Striding back along the board walk toward his office, he paused abruptly at the mouth of the narrow alley running between the hotel and the Bucket of Blood Saloon. Someone had called his name, softly, guardedly. He peered into the alley's mouth and beheld the blurred outline of a man. Hands on guns he moved closer and saw that the man was the dusty stranger he had first seen on the night of the murders.

"Come in here, Stuart, where we won't be noticed," the fellow called softly. "I got somethin' I want to talk with yuh about."

Stuart moved into the alley, narrowed eyes alert for signs of treachery.

"Well?" Stuart hinted coldly.

"I reckon you've been doin' a bit of wonderin' about me, Sheriff. I don't know as I'd blame yuh right smart if you have," the little stranger said. "I'm Kane—Ed Kane. I'm up here doin' a little lookin' round."

"Yeah?"

"Yeah—I'm lookin' for a fella what has a bad habit o' slingin' a knife when he gets riled."

"Reckon you mean the Cibecue Killer."

"That wasn't what they called him in New Mexico."

"I reckon not," said Stuart, drily. "Don't suppose you'd care to mention any names?"

"No, it don't seem hardly likely that I would," the stranger admitted, grinning.

"Just where do you fit in, Kane?"

For answer, Kane threw back his coat. Pinned to the man's vest Stuart saw a badge—a gold-plated badge. Stuart's eyes grew thoughtfully narrow.

"We been huntin' this bird for ten years," Kane spoke softly. "He's hid his tracks pretty fair but I guess likely we're gettin' close now. He left New Mexico about a jump an' a half ahead of a sheriff an' made so much dust it didn't settle all day."

"You got papers to prove that badge, I reckon," Stuart said.

Kane reached into a coat pocket and produced some which he passed across. Stuart took them and struck a match, for in the alley the shadows were still more or less murky. He glanced at the papers briefly and passed them back. "Vic Tyrone," he remarked, "is a little salty. Yuh can't never tell which way a dill pickle is apt to squirt."

"True enough," chuckled Kane, "but most hard-boiled eggs is sort of yaller inside." He peered at

Stuart through the shadows. "Besides," he said, "it ain't Vic that I'm after."

"Well, if you need any help in gettin' your man, I'd be proud to have you call on me," Stuart said as he turned away. "But I'll say this: if you an' me is after the same gent you better get a wiggle on, 'cause if I get him first this county's goin' to try him—not New Mexico!"

"Fair enough," said Kane. "I'll mebbe see you later. I'm hangin' out in the saloon here. So long," and he turned down the alley. Stuart left by the front. But no sooner had his boots touched the board walk than he stopped. Shorty Glyman was leaning against the corner of the hotel—the corner nearest the alley.

"What's the big idea, Glyman?"

"Ain't no law ag'in' leanin' on this buildin' that I ever heard of," Glyman snarled.

"Depends some on who's doin' the leaning—an' when."

"Don't get hard, Stuart. Yo're ridin' fer a fall."

"You're saddle ain't on so damned tight, either!" Stuart snapped and, turning, started up the street. Twelve steps he took, then stopped, feeling a malignant glance upon his back. So strong was the feeling it was as though someone had touched him. He swung round.

Glyman was no longer anywhere in sight. Before the hitch rail fronting the restaurant, three doors below the saloon, two men were dismounting from lathered horses; Cortaro and the boss of Flying Star. A dark scowl lay heavy on Tyrone's features; an impudent grin parted the gun fighter's lips and showed a flash of teeth. They strode into the restaurant without a word.

Swinging round once more to pursue his way, Stuart saw something he had missed before. Three horses were racked before the hotel steps beside Dorinda's—the mounts of Shelty, Jabe, and Glyman.

With eyes alert, Stuart headed for his office. The car was still parked beside the corrals, but he saw no sign of Wingate. Inside, revealed by the fiery rays of the rising sun, Stuart saw that a note was pinned to his desk with another of Margate's missing knives:

"Sherrif:

"Stop pokin into the deaths of Druce, Broughton, Campero, an the u. s. marshal fella or yores will be next on the list!
"THE KILLER OF CIBECUE."

28

As Stuart finished reading the pencil-scrawled note, Nip Wingate came striding into the office. Silently the sheriff pointed to the bit of paper. Wingate bent forward to read. Straightening with a muttered oath he turned to his superior:

"Gettin' sort of proddy. You must be close on his trail. What's he mean—the 'U. S. Marshal fella'?"

"You remember that dusty-lookin' stranger that's been hanging around town?" Stuart asked. When the other nodded, he went on: "Well, I just had a talk with him not more than twenty minutes ago. His name's Kane an' he's a U. S. Marshal sure enough. I saw his badge an' papers. He's after our killer—"

"Didn't mention the killer's name?"

Stuart grinned wryly. "Not hardly—he's out for glory an' aims to do the arrestin' personal. Where you been all night?"

"Well, I took a ride," Wingate said, and began filling his pipe from some Brown's Mule shavings which he took from his pocket. "I got that shell you wanted."

"You mean to say you been out to the Flyin' Star?"

"Wal, I been out that way," Wingate admitted, and lit his pipe. "This shell I got was fired from

262

Vic's .30-.30 all right—I can swear to that."

"You took a dang long chance, Nip. What if Vic had caught you?"

"Vic wa'n't to home, seems like. Fact is, I thought the place was deserted till I fired off that rifle. The place come to life in a hurry then. Yuh see, that ornery cook Vic's got was around someplace an' when I shot off the rifle, he come bustin' around the corner of the house with a double-barreled shotgun to his shoulder."

"Did he recognize you? Did he shoot?"

"I dunno whether he recognized me or not. I didn't ask him," Wingate expelled a cloud of smoke and added: "Take a look at the machine an' yuh can answer the last question for yourself. I ducked behind it. I brought the rifle along with me. Didn't hardly have time to put it back in the house, yuh see."

"Let's look at that shell."

Wingate placed the brass tube on the sheriff's desk. Stuart rummaged in his pockets and finally found the shell he had picked up by the corrals. Taking a magnifying glass from the drawer of his desk, he and Wingate bent above it, comparing the two shells.

"Heck," growled the deputy at last. "Looks like Vic ain't our meat after all."

Stuart's tired countenance revealed no emotion. He stood by the desk, hands deep-thrust in his pockets, his eyes brooding on the shells.

Abruptly he roused.

"Go down to that alley that cuts between the hotel an' the Bucket of Blood, Nip. See if you can get hold of that dusty stranger—there's just a chance this note's a bluff, or mebbe a bit previous. If you locate Kane, warn him that he's known an' the killer is layin' for him. Hurry!"

Wingate jammed his pipe between his teeth and departed on the run.

As his deputy's boots went flying down the walk, the something that had been bubbling in the sheriff's mind, suddenly clicked. He knew now what he had been trying to remember all night—the words of Applejack Smith: "Jabe's maw was Cal's second wife. He married Dorinda's maw first."

Stuart's jaw set hard. Jabe was at least a good four years older than the girl! What was the meaning in this difference of ages? Or was there any meaning, any significance in it?

Stuart's brooding eyes roved round the room. The black circles beneath them seemed suddenly darker, giving to his features a somber aspect not in keeping with his usual appearance. He was recalling something else, now—Wingate's story of his visit to old Jake Haskins.

With an oath, Stuart left the office, went clumping down the scarred board walk with jingling spurs. He must see Applejack Smith immediately; he must reach the livery without the loss of a single extra minute.

But, abruptly, all thoughts of Smith, his livery, and old Jake Haskins were driven from the sheriff's mind. Cortaro was lounging by the hitch rail before the restaurant. At sight of Stuart, as though he had been waiting for his appearance, the gun fighter stepped out into the dusty street.

There was no mistaking his purpose. Stuart knew that Cortaro's use to the Cibecue cowmen was about to be put to the test.

"I am about to call your bluff, señor," said the gun fighter, as Stuart drew close.

"What bluff was that?"

"The bluff about my takin' part in the gun fight. You said, señor, that eef I participate in another shooting fracas you weel run me out of this country."

"That wasn't any bluff," Stuart said, and the deep strength of him kept his face like a wooden mask. "I meant it."

Cortaro laughed, smooth and easy, his parted lips revealing his flashing teeth. The laugh was an insult, filled with scorn and contempt.

Dan Stuart chose to ignore it. "Don't be a fool, Cortaro," he said, and his hard glance was unreadable as agate.

"Bah!" Cortaro's eyes swam with mockery. "Eef you are not a frightened—pull the guns!"

Stuart's hands fell hipward.

Cortaro leaped suddenly sidewise and his hand blurred down and up. The sun glinted on the barrel of his pistol. In the empty street the roaring explosions of the heavy guns rolled up in a thudding, jarring wave of sound that slapped against the buildings on either side. Then Cortaro was reeling, staggering backward, mouth slack in a look of stunned surprise.

Twin ropes of blue smoke filtered slowly upward from the leveled guns in Stuart's hands.

Cortaro was stumbling backward like a blind man trying to catch his balance. The pistol slipped from his loosening grip. Then his knees let go and he was down, thrashing in the dusty street.

Dan Stuart felt deathly sick.

29

"For Gawd's sake, Dan, what's happened?"

That was Wingate's voice, and Stuart heard the deputy's running feet. He roused himself, looked up with haggard eyes that were like burned holes in the whiteness of his face.

"I killed Cortaro," he said lifelessly, when the puffing deputy reached his side.

Wingate stared, flung a glance at the out-sprawled figure in the dust. The pipe dropped from his sagging mouth, forgotten. The eyes he turned on Stuart were big and round. *"Cripes!"* he muttered. "Cripes!"

He stared at Stuart as though seeing him for the first time. "Cripes, it don't hardly seem possible. Jest a kid—and you downed Cortaro!"

Stuart laughed crazily.

"Gosh, Dan, don't take it like that. Git a-holt of yourself, man! We got work to do—I found that stranger in the alley, near the back door of the saloon. There was a knife stickin' in his throat!"

Wingate's blunt words shocked Stuart back to sanity. He slipped the big pistols back inside their holsters. His face was haggard, weary, bitter. Deep-etched lines ran upward from the corners of his lips to the wings of his nostrils. He looked suddenly old and tired.

"Where's Tyrone an' Jabe?"

"I ain't seen 'em," Wingate said, "nor Glyman, either. Obe Shelty's in the Bucket of Blood swillin' liquor."

Stuart nodded grimly. "Come along. We're goin' to have a talk with Applejack Smith," he gruffed, and headed for the stable.

The rising sun gilded the towering spires and rock-walled canyons of Blue House Mountain. It painted the cracks and crevices of Picture Rock in gaudy colors. It revealed the bleak spot where once Druce's tent had stood, and brightened the broad-leafed branches of the lone cottonwood above it. It also revealed the carcasses of the slaughtered steers that were piled high among the barbed wire entanglements that stretched from tree to tree.

A group of wagon bosses, herders, camp-movers and owners spread about the towering form of Bruskell in a grim half-circle. There were scowls and disapproval on many faces. But if Bruskell noticed, he paid no heed.

"Escala," he growled to his new boss herdsman, "you'll do as I say. I control this syndicate an' by—, when I give orders I intend to see 'em executed. I say turn the sheep back an' keep 'em movin'!"

Oaths and grumbling rose from the other owners. "That looks to me like a fool's move," shouted one. "That's givin' up when we got these dang cowmen on the run!"

"That's jest what we're doin'," snapped Bruskell. "We're quittin' this dang country. We bit off more'n we could chew. Escala, take yore herders an' get them sheep movin'."

"By—, I say no!" snarled another owner. "No! No! No, by—!"

"Yes! Yes! Yes, by—" Bruskell's long black eyes suddenly blazed at the insurgents. "We're clearin' out of this, an' we're clearin' out pronto! Don't lemme hear any more back talk or I'll shove a coupla gents' teeth back down their blinkin' throats! Get me? I'm bossin' this outfit an' I'll give the orders. Anybody else want to shove in their oar?"

The men fell back sullenly before Bruskell's clenched fists and fiery glance.

"Look," he growled. "Look—I thought we could beat these Cibecue cowmen, too. I thought we could get through an' cross the Rim. But I was wrong—wrong, d'ye hear? Like always, Hoskins was right. He said we'd never make it an' we won't.

"Hoskins has got a head on his shoulders. He told me las' night we'd never make it. Told me the cowmen would ruin us before we ever got halfway across the valley, an' by Cripes, Hoskins was right! These cowmen is too strong, too determined. They lost las' night, but next time they'd win. We're sellin' back to Stuart. Them as don't like it can speak up now!"

Faced by his glowering, intense black eyes and big clenched fists, no man felt the urge to speak; or if he did, wisely restrained it. There were sullen scowls, but no man spoke.

When at last the sheep were turned and the flocks went streaming out in a vast flood of dirty white and yellow, streaming out on their backward way; Bruskell sat down with the reins of his horse between his gnarled fingers and his back against the cottonwood.

One of the owners came spurring back. He questioned Bruskell's delay.

The sitting giant laughed. "Don't lag behind for me," he growled. "Vamose, an' keep them sheep on the move. I'll join you at your second camp, mebbe."

"Why not come with us now?"

"If I wanted to go with yuh now, I'd go. But I don't. I ain't quite finished in this country, yet. I got a chore to do before I leave an' come what can or will, by—, I aim to do it! Now get along with yuh an' keep them sheep a-movin'."

The man stared hard at Bruskell's crag-like figure, looked into his hard black eyes and shivered. Without further argument he left.

For long moments Bruskell sat there, opaque black eyes upon his departing flocks. First went the sheep, like a dirty, sluggish tide, then the wagons, the owners, the herders, mules and dogs. The Tucumcari Pool was on the move; the evacuation was begun.

Slowly, then, Bruskell rose to his feet, rose ponderously, as became a giant. He took the black cigar stump from his grim, red-stubbled lips; flung it away, in the direction of the slaughtered cattle. Then, mounting his waiting horse, he rode off across the range, straight into the rising sun.

30

The rising sun crept slowly higher. Bashful as a school girl it peered above the serrated crests of the White Mountains to the east of Cibecue, bending far out across the range the elongated shadow of Mount Ord.

As it slowly climbed above the peaks and bastions, it flung its golden warming beams through the open doorway of Smith's stable, flung its golden tide across the shoulders of the two lawmen who stood peering in.

As Stuart had more than half expected, they found the old man up and working, cleaning out the stalls. His long years of punching cattle for the Circle B had made his cowhand's habit of early rising hard to break.

Seeing the visitors' shadows, he looked up:

"Wal, howdy, gents. This here's a onexpected pleasure."

"I'm after a little information, Smith."

"Wal, now, Stuart, I allowed as how you likely was. Speak up—I'll do my best."

"This Cibecue was hard country in the ol' days, I take it?"

"Hard? Shucks, you don't know the haff of it! Tobacco juice an' lightnin'!"

Wingate grinned. "It ain't so dawgone tame right now," he hinted.

"Wal, mebbe not. But it shore don't hold a candle to what it was when I was a young 'un," Smith said pridefully. He turned back to Stuart. "I reckon you are wantin' to hear about the Kelvans, ain't yuh? I been sorta figgerin' you might be back ag'in."

"You just do the talkin'," Stuart said grimly. "I came to listen. Talk about any of the old doings that you think might be of interest to us. If I get bored I'll stop you."

"Ho-ho!" Smith chuckled. "I can guarantee yuh won't get bored. Wal, peel yore ears, gents—here goes: Them Kelvans was a queer bunch—come from some place over in New Mexico. They was up to Holbrook fer a spell; Miz Kelvan, she run a hash house. The Ol' Man used tuh ship his cattle from Holbrook every year. I recollect the first time he set eyes on her he seemed tuh get a heap interested. Got so he couldn't hardly keep away from that dang hash house long enough tuh tend to business. But we got the cattle loaded after a fashion. He gave us boys a coupla days tuh spree around an' then sent us home. Said he'd be along later.

"Wal, we could all see he was pretty far gone on the boss of the Kelvan hash house. A fella couldn't hardly blame him, though. She had a right pert good-lookin' pair o' eyes an' a good

273

figger. Besides, she was pretty as a little red wagon. A gay widder, an' no mistake—as the sayin' goes. An' like I say, a fella couldn't hardly blame him none. Most any gent would get a heap lonely with no one round the house fer eight years but a kid girl an' a ol' Mex woman tuh do the cookin'.

"Wal, the upshot of it was that when he come shaggin' along home, he had Miz Kelvan an' young Kelvan in tow. He an' she had got hitched up. Things went along smooth as butter fer a—"

"Just a second," Stuart cut in. "You got any notion why they left New Mexico?"

"Them Kelvans? Uh, let's see, now—" Smith removed his disreputable hat to run a gnarled hand through the clump of silvery hair that adorned his otherwise-bald head like an Indian warlock. He chewed his tobacco reflectively; his puckered eyes held a faraway look and his brows were knit in ponderous thought. He spat at a knothole in the floor and spoke:

"Wal, it seems tuh me there was a story goin' round thet they had owned a small cow spread. As I recollect it, some sheepmen was tryin' tuh grab the range. Bein' small owners, I reckon they figgered as how the Kelvans' was a right smart place tuh make a start. The way I heard it, they burned the buildin's one shady night, run off the stock an' left ol' Kelvan with a knife in his back—"

"Cripes!" Wingate scowled. "I allus said Vic Tyrone was a ornery gent!"

"Shucks, color don't count fer much if the colt don't trot," Applejack Smith replied. "Like I was sayin', they left ol' Kelvan with a knife in his back—"

"I reckon," Stuart's voice was low, cold, even; "we've heard about enough."

His faded, disreputable Levi's were full of wrinkles, his boots were scuffed and dusty. His pinto vest hung open, disclosing beneath it the dark, crossed gun belts with their shiny rows of brass cartridges and their sagging tied-down holsters.

One at a time he removed his pistols from their greasy leathers and, extracting the spent shells from their chambers, replaced them with fresh cartridges from his belts. His lean square jaw was grim and the lips above it held a tight, determined look that boded ill for someone.

"Come on, Nip," he seemed to have forgotten the watching stableman, "we're goin' over to the Warwhoop. There's a party stayin' there I want to talk to." He looked at Wingate appraisingly. He appeared to come to some decision. "Let's go."

As Stuart and Nip Wingate entered the dingy lobby of the Warwhoop Hotel the proprietor looked up from behind the counter and, seeing them, scowled.

"Lost somethin'?" the eyes behind his thick-lensed spectacles were cold.

But they were no colder than the sheriff's low voice: "Gantley, which room is Miss Broughton stayin' in?"

"So the law in these parts has slumped so low it's pickin' on women, now, eh?"

"I've stood about all I intend to outa you, Gantley," Stuart drawled. "I asked which room was Miss Broughton's."

The proprietor was daunted by the sheriff's unwavering glance. "She ain't stayin' here," he answered, sullenly.

"Don't lie to me. I left her here not more than an hour ago."

"I'm tellin' you the truth, sheriff. She ain't here any more. Her brother came in a short time after she did an' pretty soon they left together. Vic Tyrone was with 'em."

"Did she check out?"

"Wal, no. She said she wanted to keep her room, but she left the keys with me."

"She's coming back, is she?"

"Why, yes, I reckon she is. She said she was keepin' the room—paid a week in advance. By check."

The sheriff was thinking. Dorinda had told him to come to the hotel and she would tell him how her handkerchief came to be found in the camp at Picture Rock. Perhaps she had left a note for him in her room. "Let's have the key, Gantley. Which room is it?"

"You got a search warrant?" Gantley's pale eyes shifted uneasily behind their thick-lensed spectacles.

"You know I haven't. What's more, it won't be necessary. You can tag along if you want—but I'm goin' to see the inside of that room. Now!"

Gantley muttered under his breath, but produced the key and led the way. The girl's room was on the second floor.

While the men were on their way up the narrow wooden stairs, that creaked at each and every step, a startled cry rang out. It was in a girl's voice and it came from the second floor corridor.

Gantley winched at the sound.

"What the heck!" Nip Wingate growled.

Shoving the others unceremoniously aside, Stuart darted up the stairs. Reaching the second floor he came to a dead stop, staring. Gantley's girl-of-all-work stood rigid in the center of the corridor, before an open door. One hand was at her lips and her eyes were bulging, filled with horror.

When she saw the sheriff she let out a second shriek and started fleeing down the hall.

"Stop!" Stuart shouted, and the girl ceased her headlong flight as though a ghost had risen in her path. "Come back here," said Stuart, advancing toward the open door, Gantley and Wingate crowding at his back. "Nobody's goin' to hurt

you, but I want you to stick around till I find out what that cry was for. Somebody get fresh with you?"

"N-n-no!" she stammered, and shook her head dazedly.

"What did you cry out for, then? Who's got that room?" he pointed to the room with the open door.

"No one's got it," Gantley snapped. "The room's empty. Probably she was tidyin' up in there."

The girl nodded, having got control of herself under the sheriff's questioning. "Yes, the door was unlocked—when the rooms are empty we always keep them unlocked—and I went in to see if things needed straightening up. I—I—"

"What's in there, then, to scare you?" Stuart started toward the door.

The girl's face was very white, her voice was hardly louder than a whisper:

"There's a dead man in there—a man with a knife in his back. He's layin' on the bed an' there's blood all over—"

At a bound the sheriff reached the door, the others crowding in behind him. As the girl had said, a man was lying on the bed and there was a knife that looked like one of Margate's missing six sticking hilt-deep in his back. He had been dead for several hours.

"So that's where he went," the sheriff murmured, grim eyes upon the bed.

"My Gawd, Dan," Wingate whispered, "it's Haines!"

"Yeah." Stuart's face was taut, masklike. "I was afraid the killer might've spotted him when he came to the office yesterday. He certainly saw him with you last night. Once you left him, the killer must've lured him here somehow. He didn't lose no time."

He rose from his hasty examination. "He's been dead fourteen or fifteen hours, I'd say. Probably the killer stabbed him as soon as he got him in this room."

"What are we gonna do, Dan?"

"Do? We're goin' to get this knife-slingin' buzzard," Stuart said through tight lips. "An' we're goin' to get him quick."

"But who—?"

"Ain't you guessed who he is yet, Nip?"

"I expect I'm uncommon dumb," Wingate confessed, rasping his unshaven chin. "But I can't hardly say as I have—unless it's Vic Tyrone."

Stuart stood by the bed, hands deep-thrust in his pockets, his eyes brooding on the recumbent figure of the dead rancher.

"I got a hunch Bruskell's headin' for the Circle B," he said, and swung toward the door. He had to beat the man to the ranch if he could. No telling what might happen to Dorinda with the Cibecue knifeman on the warpath. Stuart had small doubt but that the ranch was where Jabe had gone with her. If Bruskell got there before him there was no guessing the result. But someone would most certainly die, he told himself.

"Nip, get busy pronto an' round up four or five fellows you can trust—fellows that you know can be depended on to sling a gun with sure results. Deputize 'em an' load 'em in the machine. Hit for the Circle B." He wished he dare take the car himself, but knew that it would double the girl's hazard if he did. For he aimed to beat Wingate and his posse and if the killer should down him, those deputies would need be close at hand to save the girl.

Out the door he flung himself and down the narrow hall.

"Where you goin'?" Wingate yelled.

"Circle B!" Stuart went plunging down the steps.

31

An atmosphere of intense quiet hung over the ranch headquarters of the Circle B. Four horses with downflung heads and spraddled legs stood tethered to the split pole fence near the corrals. These animals afforded the only sign of animation to be detected in the aspen-bordered clearing. The corrals loomed bleak and empty, their gates thrown wide. No smoke curled upward from the protruding stovepipe that towered above the cookshack roof.

At the far end of the tree-shaded lane leading to the ranch house, Stuart had left his horse. Cautiously he had inched his way forward until now he lay crouched by a corner of the foreman's shanty. He was satisfied the building was empty. The cookshack and bunkhouse were apparently in the same condition. The four horses standing tethered to the fence belonged to Dorinda, Jabe, Vic Tyrone and Bruskell. He had groaned at sight of the latter's horse. That further blood had been spilled already, he did not doubt.

He had made the best time possible to a man on horseback, having taken several short cuts out of the question for men traveling in a machine, as was the posse under Wingate. Nevertheless, Bruskell had gotten here first.

The wide veranda fronting the earth-roofed ranch house was devoid of life. No sound came drifting from the long main room behind it. Yet Stuart, crouched by the foreman's shanty, felt certain that of the four whose horses were hitched to the fence, at least one must be yet alive.

He glanced at his shadow, found that it was nearly eight o'clock. The broad beams of the morning sun slanted down upon the clearing hotly, warmed the boards of the wide veranda but did not penetrate the open ranch house door.

The place might look deserted, but Stuart did not aim to make any foolish moves until he knew. He was well aware of the deceptive nature of appearances. Eternal vigilance was the price of life in the desert country. None knew it better than the sheriff.

No faintest twittering of birds came down to him from the trembling foliage of the aspens, no sign of movement other than the shaking of the leaves. A brooding hush, wherein lurked a strong-felt tenseness, gripped the clearing.

Stuart wondered if he had been seen as he inched his way forward among the trees. He hardly thought it likely for he had used every conceivable precaution. He decided to wait another five minutes for some sound or movement about the house. If none came within that time, he would— Well, he did not know what he would do, but he would do something—that much was certain.

He sensed a metallic quality to the stillness, as though it were a brittle thing. There was the feel of impending tragedy in the heating air; a thing plainly apprehended but, like Destiny or Death, neither to be prevented nor avoided.

Abruptly he caught a low mutter of conversation. It seemed to come from the open ranch house door. He could not make out the words but the tone was unmistakable—threatening. In the brief pause that followed, Stuart slipped the spurs from his booted heels and prepared for action.

Bruskell's gruff voice broke the silence. His tone was sneering:

"Look—you'll never talk me out of it. You're done, yuh fool! Washed up!"

Dorinda screamed.

Stuart crossed the clearing in eight swift bounds, struck the veranda, grated to a stop before the door. The light inside was dull in shocking contrast to the brilliant sunlight of the yard. For the several moments he hung motionless in the doorway, he could see but dimly the figures grouped inside. Then he was striding forward and his voice was sharp:

"Bruskell!"

He saw the man's stolid, unemotional beefy face, his heavy-lidded eyes and grim, unsmiling lips. And more.

In the single fleeting glance with which he

raked the room, Stuart saw that Bruskell and the girl were lashed to chairs. Saw that Vic Tyrone lounged grinning against the farther wall, the thumb of his right hand hooked in his cartridge belt within swift reach of his gun.

The dry laugh that rattled suddenly across young Broughton's lips was startling in the brittle hush that was complete save for the low, distant whine of an approaching motor.

Stuart hung motionless, his face a shadowed mask. The words that issued from his barely-moving lips were like drops of water falling on a heated stone:

"I'm arrestin' you, Jabe Kelvan Broughton, for the murders of Druce, Big Cal, Campero, Kane and Haines."

For a single long-drawn second the silence held.

Jabe's sneering lips writhed back from his yellowed teeth as Stuart's upper body drooped forward in a half-crouch, heart pounding, his spine a-tingle with anticipation of nearing death, of roaring guns and the searing bite of lead.

Jabe's high-boned face hung dark and sinister in the dusky room. Light flared abruptly in his smouldering eyes and his hands dropped toward his holsters.

No expression marked the sheriff's taut features. No twitching muscle conveyed to the others the bitter hatefulness of the task before him. Jabe deserved death many times over, yet that made the coming fight no less distasteful in Stuart's eyes. He caught the rip of steel on leather as Jabe and Tyrone drew.

The big guns rocked against his palms.

Bursting explosions choked the room with sullen thunder. The criss-cross streaks of gun-flame were like lightning in the dimness. The place stank with the acrid fumes of gunpowder.

As lead smacked the door frame behind him, Stuart saw a dark spot break out on the whiteness of Tyrone's forehead; saw him stagger back against the wall, slide down it to the floor and crumple.

Jabe's right arm, as it raised with a gun, was jerked aside—thrown out of line by the impact of Stuart's lead. But the gun went off; spoke once as Jabe, hurled sideways by a bullet in his thigh, struck a table and carried it down in a splintering crash as he went to the floor.

Stuart's guns kicked back again in sharp recoil and the pistol in Jabe's left hand went slithering across the room. He cursed in pain and fury and, clawing his way to where his other pistol had fallen, picked it up and flipped it level as Stuart's guns spoke again.

Jabe's snarling features distorted with incredulity and rage. He swayed there on one elbow, eyes blazing, still striving to pull the trigger, though its muzzle now pointed at the floor.

Slowly the rage receded from his features and

only the incredulity remained. Gradually his eyes mirrored the realization that he was whipped, that death was close. Then his gaze grew blank and glassy. His elbow slid from under him, left him motionless and limp.

As Stuart finished cutting the ropes that bound Dorinda and Bruskell to their chairs, the doorway filled with faces, struggling bodies, as the posse excitedly crowded in.

Stuart turned to face them.

"Good Gawd! What's come off here?" Wingate gasped.

The sheriff's face was haggard, drawn and weary. "It's over, boys. The killer's dead."

"So it *was* Vic Tyrone!" gulped the deputy.

"No—Jabe Broughton," Stuart said. "Vic was only a two-bit rustler, but he stacked up man-size when I called Jabe's hand. He got in first shot—you'll find his bullets in the door frame. It's over, boys. You can pack these fellas in to town."

"Cripes," Nip Wingate muttered, "I'd like tuh hear the story!"

"It's brief an' soon told," Stuart answered. "Dorinda will correct me if I'm wrong.

"Ten years or so ago in New Mexico, a bunch of sheepmen made a play to get them a bigger reach of range, said range bein' grazed at the time by cowmen. They opened up the game by goin' after a small owner by the name of Kelvan. They raided his place one night, burned the buildings and scared off the stock. Kelvan was struck down by a knife. Kelvan's young son, Jabe, saw the killin' an' the man that did it. That man was Caspar Druce.

"In the range war that followed, young Jabe and his mother pulled stakes and came to Arizona, settling in Holbrook where Mrs. Kelvan opened up a restaurant. A short time later Big Cal Broughton, in Holbrook with a herd of beef, met her, liked her, and—his own wife having been dead a matter of eight or nine years—married her. She and young Jabe came back with him to Cibecue where Jabe took Broughton's name.

"As time went on Jabe showed signs of a vindictive, vengeful nature and Dorinda, who had heard the story, watched him covertly after his mother's death.

"This year, when I was elected sheriff, I decided to devote all my time to that job, and as prices for beef were nothing to brag about I advertised my ranch for sale. A man named Hoskins, claiming himself secretary to the Tucumcari Pool—which I naturally supposed was a cattle syndicate—wrote me and said he was coming on to look the property over. He came and finally bought, on behalf of his association.

"From time to time I heard rumors of the changes he was making in the ranch. But not until I heard sheep were at Picture Rock did I begin to realize I'd been tricked. I came to Cibecue pronto, determined to prevent the war my careless sale of the S Bar 4 seemed likely to provoke. I went at once to Druce and offered to buy the ranch back at once-and-a-half the price paid. He laughed at me. There was nothing left for me to do but strive to keep the sheep and cattle interests from clashing.

"But Jabe, too, was interested in the sheepmen. I imagine he skulked around their camp nights until he saw and recognized Druce. He determined to kill the man—to kill him in the same manner as Druce had killed his father. He left this ranch night before last with that set purpose. But Dorinda, having seen him set off toward Picture Rock several nights previous, and knowing his vengeful nature an' the story of his father's death by a man named Druce, got her horse and followed him."

He paused to glance at the girl's white face.

"Yes," Dorinda said. "I followed him. But I lost him just this side of Picture Rock and did not see him again that night. For a while I circled round trying to locate him, but at last, seeing the futility of my aimless riding, I went on to the sheepmen's camp. It seemed deserted but I saw a lighted tent and rode toward it.

"When I got close, I saw the form of a man sprawled before it on the ground. I was frightened. But I was curious, too. I got off my horse and, bending above him, turned him over. There was a narrow wound, as though made by a knife, in his back. I was sure it had been made by a knife because his coat and shirt were slashed.

"I grew panicky. It must have been then that I dropped my handkerchief. I had been following Jabe toward the camp. I had lost him in the darkness. Then when I arrived in camp, I found this man dead before his tent. It seemed that the only possible answer must spell Jabe.

"I got on my horse somehow and rode blindly. After a time I realized that I had ought to tell my father so I turned the horse toward town. I found him and told him what I had done and seen and of my suspicions that it was Jabe."

"What did Big Cal say?" asked Stuart gently.

"He didn't say anything for a time. He just looked sort of—sort of sick. Then he said we'd ought to know which side you'd take in case of a range war resulting from Druce's murder. He asked me to sound you out." She looked at him reproachfully. "You remember—you wouldn't say?"

Stuart nodded. "I couldn't have said. I was determined not to take sides; I did not intend to let things come to such a pass that taking sides would be necessary. I had sold land to the sheepmen, thus bringing them into the country. If men died in a sheep and cattle war, *I* would be the one to blame. I was prepared to lose my life, if necessary, to prevent such a situation from occurring."

"Yeah, we can see your point, Dan," Wingate said impatiently. "But what about Jabe—what did he do after killin' Druce?"

"He must have headed for town immediately to make himself an alibi. Probably slipped in the back door of the Bucket of Blood and strove to create the impression he'd been there all evenin'. He was not there when I entered after Dorinda left the office, however. While Dorinda was visiting me, I think he went outside to talk with Big Cal. At any rate, I am satisfied in my own mind that about that time he and Big Cal somehow got together and the old man accused Jabe of killin' Druce.

"Jabe knew that he'd be a goner unless he silenced his foster-father swiftly. He stabbed him either in the alley, or else he stabbed him someplace else and dragged the old man's body into the alley to conceal it. But he was in a hurry; probably afraid he would be missed by those in the saloon. He forgot to remove his knife from the body.

"But Big Cal wasn't quite dead. He groaned once or twice just as I came walking past the mouth of the alley. I suspected it was a trap at first, until I saw Jabe's shadowy figure slipping through the shadows at the alley's farther end. I couldn't recognize him in the darkness—all I could see was a moving shadow.

"I ran down the alley and struck a match. I saw that it was Big Cal who lay there. Jabe saw my match flare and took a shot at me, but missed. I ran after him. When I got to the back of the alley the crowd in the saloon came running out, attracted by the shots. Jabe was among them. He'd pulled some mighty fast work, or else he'd joined them unobserved as they came rushing out.

"Possibly Jabe hadn't been in the saloon before he met and killed Big Cal. I don't know. He might have been slipping down the alley, hoping to enter the Bucket of Blood without bein' seen, and suddenly found himself face to face with Big Cal. Only the old man's prompt accusation would account for Jabe killin' him. Big Cal had done a heap for Jabe—but that wouldn't save him if Jabe thought the old man meant to place a rope around his neck. I think Jabe struck him in panic as the old fellow turned away."

"Cripes!" Wingate grunted. "But how'n heck did yuh ever come to suspicion Jabe in the first place. *I* never thought he was the killer—I'd have bet my shirt 'twas Vic Tyrone!"

"In the first place," said Stuart, wearily, "I knew Dorinda's handkerchief had been found in the sheepmen's camp that night."

"Shucks, yes—but I knew that, too."

"So did Bruskell," Stuart answered, "an' Bruskell thought it was Jabe— He come out here to get him, but he didn't have much luck."

The sheepman nodded grimly. "I didn't know that story about Kelvan, but I guessed as much, puttin' together a number of things I did know," he told them.

Swiftly then, Stuart ran over the case point by point from the time he had found the body of Big Cal Broughton in the alley between the Bucket of Blood and the Warwhoop Hotel. He pointed out that each man killed after the murder of Druce, had been killed through fear that they had known something and would probably talk.

"But I hadn't really settled on Jabe as bein' the guilty man," he concluded, "until I remembered that Applejack Smith had told me Jabe's mother had been Cal's second wife, an' that Cal had married Dorinda's mother first.

"Thinkin' that over more carefully, it seemed kind of queer to me that Jabe was older than Dorinda. I recalled then what ol' Jake Haskins had told Wingate when he went up to Standard to see him—that Jabe was not Big Cal's son.

"I talked with the stranger, Marshal Kane, just before he was murdered by Jabe—who was likely listenin' to us—an' he told me that he'd been trailin' Druce for some time. That he had lit out of New Mexico pretty fast right after the killin' of Kelvan—though he didn't mention Kelvan by name, of course. In fact he refused to mention names. When he at last caught up with

Druce, who didn't stay with his outfits more than a week or so at a time, an' found him dead, Kane naturally decided to turn his attention to Druce's killer. I hinted that Vic was a hard gent to monkey with. Kane grinned an' said he wasn't after Vic.

"That left me two possibilities—the Cibecue knifeman was either Bruskell, here, or Jabe. And I was pretty certain it wasn't Bruskell.

"Like you remember, Nip, you an' me went down to talk with Smith this mornin'. He told us how ol' man Kelvan was murdered by a sheepman an' how the Kelvans came to be mixed up with the Broughtons. I knew then that Jabe was the Killer of Cibecue."

After Nip Wingate and the posse had departed in the machine, taking with them the bodies of Jabe and Tyrone, Bruskell stood up and, reaching inside his coat pocket, produced a legal-appearing document which he gravely handed the sheriff.

Stuart took it and saw that it was the deed to the S Bar 4. He shook Bruskell's ham-like hand. "I'm glad you're showin' good sense," he told him.

Bruskell grinned. "You can make me out a check for that when you get to town. Just what Druce paid you, Stuart—the straight amount. I'll be waitin' at your office." He looked at the sheriff whimsically. "It's plain this ain't sheepmen's country. I'll be glad to get its dust off'n my boots."

"Hold on a second," Stuart said. "I'll make out a check for you now."

Bruskell chuckled. "My maw told me at a tender age that two was always plenty company—three, one fella too many!" and, with a bow to Dorinda, he went striding out the door.